His eyes lifted to her lips and she didn't breathe—she couldn't—for several long seconds.

Her lungs burned.

He was going to kiss her. His eyes were so intent on her lips, his body so close—when had that even happened?—his expression so loaded with sensuality that memories weaved through her, reminding her of what they'd shared.

She waited, her face upturned, her lips parted, her blood firing so hard and fast that she could barely think, let alone hear. She knew she should step backward, move away from him—this was all too complicated—but she couldn't. She wouldn't. Just as the hand of fate seemed to guide them in the maze, a far greater force was at work now.

She expelled a shuddering breath simply because her lungs needed to work, and with the exhalation, her body swayed forward a little, not intentionally and not by much, but it brought her to him.

"Johara."

Dear Reader,

Romeo and Juliet is an enduring love story, though there is no happily-ever-after for the characters. Quite the opposite. This long-lived play is a cautionary tale, a warning against hatred and rivalry, a reminder that nothing good can come from blind acrimony.

When I came to write *Their Impossible Desert Match*, I knew I wanted to write a modern retelling of *Romeo and Juliet*—but without the death! Whenever I've read or seen a performance of this classic, I've always crossed my fingers and hoped that perhaps the ending would be different this time. Writing *Their Impossible Desert Match* was my chance to make that wish come true! This is my own version of this classic love story, with my own spin, but as I wrote it I was mindful of wanting the book to hold fast to the themes of Shakespeare's classic—to serve as a reminder that tolerance and peace will always serve us better than anger and enmity.

I hope you enjoy reading Amir and Johara's story as much as I loved writing it.

Happy reading.

Love,

Clare

Clare Connelly

THEIR IMPOSSIBLE DESERT MATCH

HARLEQUIN
PRESENTS

HARLEQUIN®
PRESENTS®

Recycling programs
for this product may
not exist in your area.

ISBN-13: 978-1-335-89408-3

Their Impossible Desert Match

Copyright © 2020 by Clare Connelly

This edition published by arrangement with Harlequin Books S.A.

For questions and comments about the quality of this book,
please contact us at CustomerService@Harlequin.com.

Harlequin Enterprises ULC
22 Adelaide St. West, 40th Floor
Toronto, Ontario M5H 4E3, Canada
www.Harlequin.com

Printed in U.S.A.

Clare Connelly was raised in small-town Australia among a family of avid readers. She spent much of her childhood up a tree, Harlequin book in hand. Clare is married to her own real-life hero, and they live in a bungalow near the sea with their two children. She is frequently found staring into space—a surefire sign she is in the world of her characters. She has a penchant for French food and ice-cold champagne, and Harlequin novels continue to be her favorite-ever books. Writing for Harlequin Presents is a long-held dream. Clare can be contacted via clareconnelly.com or on her Facebook page.

Books by Clare Connelly

Harlequin Presents

Innocent in the Billionaire's Bed
Her Wedding Night Surrender
Bound by the Billionaire's Vows
Spaniard's Baby of Revenge
Redemption of the Untamed Italian
The Secret Kept from the King
Hired by the Impossible Greek

Secret Heirs of Billionaires

Shock Heir for the King

Christmas Seductions

Bound by Their Christmas Baby
The Season to Sin

Crazy Rich Greek Weddings

The Greek's Billion-Dollar Baby
Bride Behind the Billion-Dollar Veil

Visit the Author Profile page
at Harlequin.com for more titles.

PROLOGUE

Nineteen years ago. The Royal Palace of Ishkana, on the edge of the Al'amani ranges.

'TELL ME IMMEDIATELY.' It didn't matter to His Royal Highness Prince Amir Haddad that he was just twelve and the advisors in his bedroom were all at least three times that in age. From birth he had been raised to know his place in the kingdom, the duty that would one day be his.

Having six men sweep into his private quarters at four in the morning might have caused a ripple of anxiety deep in his gut, but he revealed nothing. His dark eyes fixed on advisor Ahmed, one of his father's most trusted servants, and he waited quietly, with an unintended look of steel in his eyes.

Ahmed took a step forward, deeper into Amir's bedroom. Ancient tapestries adorned the walls and a blade of moonlight caught one, drawing Amir's attention for a moment to the silver and blue threads that formed an image of the country's ancient western aqueducts. He felt that he should stand up, face whatever was coming with his eyes open, and so he did, pushing back sheets made of the finest linen, pressing his feet to the mosaics—gold and blue and green, they swirled like water and flame beneath him. At twelve, he was almost as tall as any of the men present.

'Tell me,' he repeated, the quality of steel shifting from his eyes to his voice.

Ahmed nodded slowly, swallowing so his Adam's apple shifted visibly. 'There was an attack, Your Highness.'

Amir waited.

'Your parents' convoy was targeted.'

Amir's only response was to straighten his spine; he continued to stare at Ahmed, his young face symmetrical and intent. Inside, his stomach was in knots and ice was flooding his veins.

'They were hurt?'

He heard one of the other servants groan, but he didn't take his eyes off Ahmed. With Ahmed he felt a degree of comfort; he trusted him.

'Yes. They were badly hurt.' Ahmed cleared his throat, his gentle features showing anguish. He put a hand on Amir's shoulder—a contact that was unprecedented. 'Amir, they were killed.'

The words were delivered with compassion and a pain all of his own—Ahmed had served Amir's father for a very long time, since he himself was a boy. The pain he felt must have run deep.

Amir nodded, understanding, knowing he would need to deal with his grief later, when he was alone. Only then he would allow his pain to run through his body, felling him to his knees for what he had lost. He wouldn't mourn publicly; that was not his way, and it was not what his country required of him. How long had that message been instilled in his heart? He was now his country's King, his people's servant.

'By whom?'

One of the other servants stood forward. Amir recognised the military medals he wore across the breast of his white uniform. He had a thick moustache, black and long. 'A band of renegades from Taquul.'

Amir's eyes closed for a moment. The country directly to the east, with whom Ishkana had been embroiled in bitter unrest for over a century. How many lives had been lost because of it? And now his parents were gone.

He, Amir, was Sheikh of Ishkana.

'A band of renegades,' Ahmed continued gently, 'led by His Highness Johar Qadir.'

Amir dug his hands into his hips, rocked on his heels, and nodded slowly. The King of Taquul's brother was a well-documented troublemaker. It was known that he sympathised with the people who inhabited the borders of their two lands, a people who had benefited for years from the ongoing conflict and wanted it to continue, at all costs. But this?

This was a step further. This was a new twist in the century-old war, one that was unforgivable. And for as long as he lived, Amir would make the Qadirs pay. He hated them with a vengeance that nothing—and no one—could ever quell.

CHAPTER ONE

Princess Johara Qadir cut through the room with an innate elegance, pleased the evening was a masquerade for the anonymity it afforded her. The delicately constructed mask she'd been given to wear was made of onyx and pearl, with diamonds around the eyes and ostrich feathers on one side, which rose at least two feet above her head. The mask concealed everything but her eyes and lips, meaning she could pass unrecognised on this evening to all but those who knew her very, very well and could recognise the sparkle that lit the depths of her golden brown eyes.

'You have no choice, Johara. The whole family must appear to be united behind this decision. For our people...'

Yes, for their people. The prospect of peace with neighbouring Ishkana meant too much, would save lives, improve safety and lifestyle— of course she must support her brother's decision to enter a treaty with the neighbouring Sheikh.

It wasn't that that bothered her.

It was being summoned to return to the kingdom—for good. To leave behind her life in New York, the important work she was doing to support childhood literacy; it was leaving behind the identity she'd carved out for herself there. And for what? To come home to Taquul where her future was all mapped out for her? A ceremonial title and marriage to the man her brother deemed most suitable, Paris Alkad'r? A role in this kingdom as ornamental but useless and ineffective?

It felt like a form of suffocation to even contemplate that kind of life and yet she understood her over-protective brother's thinking. He'd seen the way she'd been after Matthew— the American she'd fallen in love with and who had broken her heart. The newspaper articles had been relentless, the tabloids delighting in her pain. Malik wanted to spare her that—but an arranged marriage was about ten steps too far. Besides, the kind of marriage he and Paris envisaged—a political alliance—was the last thing she wanted!

A spirit of rebellion fired inside her.

Her brother was the Sheikh. He was older, true, but, more importantly, he had been raised to rule a country. Johara's importance—compared to his—had never been considered as particularly great—at least, not by their parents. Even Malik seemed, at times, to forget that she was a person with her own free will, simply snapping his fingers and expecting her to jump. Her closest friend in New York had commiserated and said that it was the same with her and her older sister—'older siblings are always bossy as hell'—but Johara doubted anyone could match the arrogance of Malik. She adored him, but that didn't mean she wasn't capable of feeling enraged by his choices, at times.

She expelled a sigh, took a glass of champagne from a passing waitress and had a small sip, then replaced it on another waitress's tray. Every detail of the party was exquisite. The National Ballet were serving as wait staff, each ballerina dressed in a pale pink and silver tutu, dancing as they moved through the crowd, mesmerising, beautiful, enchanting. The enormous marble hall had been opened for the occasion— showcasing the wealth and ancient prestige of the country, the windows displaying views of the desert in one direction and the Al'amanï ranges in the other. Large white marble steps led to an enormous lagoon; man-made, centuries ago, it had a free-form shape and was lit with small fires all around it. Glass had been carefully laid over the edges, allowing guests to hover over the water. Gymnasts danced in the water, their synchronised routines drawing gasps from those who stood outside. Fairy lights were strung overhead, casting a beautiful, 'midsummer night's dream' feeling.

Nothing had been missed.

Another sigh escaped Johara's lips. In New York, she had still been a princess, and the trappings of home had, of course, followed her. She'd had bodyguards who accompanied her discreetly wherever she went, she'd stayed at a royal apartment, and from time to time had taken part in official functions. However, she had been, by and large, free to live her own life.

Could she really give that up to come home and be, simply, ornamental? What about her burning desire to be of use?

Her eyes flicked across the room. Dignitaries from all corners of the globe had travelled to Taquul for this momentous occasion—an occasion most said would never happen. Peace between Ishkana and Taquul was almost an oxymoron, despite the fact the war had raged for so long that it had become a habit rather than anything else. A foreign diplomat was strutting proudly, evidently congratulating himself on bringing about this tentative peace accord. Johara's lips twisted into an enigmatic smile. Little did the diplomat know, no one could force her brother into anything that was not his desire.

He wanted this peace. He knew it was time. The ancient enmity had been a part of their life for generations, but it didn't serve the people. The hatred was dangerous and it was purpose-less. How many more people had to die?

Perhaps in the beginning it served its pur-pose. The landscapes of Ishkana and Taquul were inhospitable. True, there was beauty and there was plenty in parts, but not enough, and the regions that had been in dispute a hundred years ago were those most plentiful with water, most arable and productive. Though a property accord had been reached, the war had continued and the accord had always seemed dangerously close to falling through. Add to that a group of tribes in the mountains who wanted independ-ence from both countries, who worked to en-sure the mistrust and violence continued, and Johara could only feel surprise that this peace had finally been wrought. Detailed negotiations between both countries and an agreement to im-pose strict laws on both sides of the mountains had led to this historic, hopeful event.

She hoped, more than anything, the peace would last.

'You are bored.' A voice cut through her thoughts, drawing her gaze sideways. A man had moved to stand at her side. He wore a mask over the top half of his face—soft velvet, it hugged the contours of his features, so she could still discern the strength and symmetry that lay beneath. A jaw that was squared, a nose that was strong and angular, and lips that were masculine yet full. His hair was dark as the depths of the ocean might be, and just as mesmerising—thick with a natural wave, it was cut to the collar of his robe and, though it was neat, she had the strangest feeling it was suppressed wildness, that it wanted to be long and loose, free of restraint. His eyes were dark like flint, and his body was broad, muscular, tall, as though cast in the image of an ancient idol. The thought came to her out of nowhere and sent a shiver pulsing down her spine. He wore an immaculate robe, black with gold at the cuffs and collar, complementing the mask on his face. He looked…mysterious and fascinating.

Dangerous.

He looked temptingly like the rebellion she wanted to stage, so she forced herself to look away while she still could.

'Not at all.' She was unrecognisable as the Princess of Taquul, but that didn't mean she could speak as freely as she wanted. And not to a stranger.

But she felt his eyes on her, watching her,

and an inexplicable heat began to simmer inside her veins. She kept looking forward. 'There is somewhere else you'd rather be though?' he prompted, apparently not letting his curiosity subside.

She felt a burst of something shake her, willing her to speak to him, to be honest.

'I—' She swallowed, tilting her gaze towards him. The mask emboldened her. She was hidden, secret. He didn't know who she was, and she had no idea who he was. They were simply two strangers at a state function. No rank, no names. A smile curved slowly over her lips. 'Up until twenty hours ago, I was in Manhattan.' She lifted her shoulders, conscious of the way the delicate gown moved with her.

'And you would prefer to be there.'

'It is a momentous occasion.' She gestured around the room, then turned back to face him fully. 'Everyone in Taquul will be rejoicing at the prospect of peace with Ishkana after so long.'

His eyes gave little away; they were stony and cool. 'Not everyone.'

'No?'

'There are many who will harbour hatred and resentment for their lifetimes. Peace does not come about because two men snap their fingers and decide it should.'

Fascination fluttered inside her. 'You don't think people see the sense in peace?'

His lips curved in an approximation of a smile. There was something about its innate cynicism that sparked a fire in her blood. 'Ah, then we are talking about sense and not feeling. What one feels often has very little to do with what one thinks.'

Surprise hitched in her throat. It was an interesting and perceptive observation; she found herself more interested in him than she'd expected to be by anyone at this event. She took a small step without realising it, then another, leading them around the edges of the space.

'Nonetheless, I believe the people of Taquul will feel enormous relief, particularly those in the border regions. What's needed is a unified front to quell the unease in the mountain ranges.'

His eyes burned her with their intensity—strange when a moment ago she'd been thinking how like cool stone they were.

'Perhaps.'

'You don't agree?'

His lips curved in another mocking smile. 'I do not think peace can be so easily achieved.'

'I hope you're wrong.'

'I doubt it.'

She laughed; she couldn't help it. His cyni-

cism was so completely natural, as though he
barely realised he was doing it.

'I believe people can obey a peace treaty,'
he said quietly, his voice dark. 'But that hatred
dies a long, slow death. Many lives have been
lost on both sides. How many deaths have there
been in this war? Would you not wish to retali-
ate against a man who murdered someone you
loved?'

Sadness brushed through her at his words and
she couldn't help wondering if he'd lost someone
to the awful unrest of their people. 'I think vigi-
lantism is bad for that very reason. It's why vic-
tims should never get to enact retribution—how
easy it would be to answer death with death,
pain with pain, instead of finding the restor-
ative properties of forgiveness.'

He was silent; she couldn't tell if he agreed
or not, only that he was thinking. They reached
the edge of the enormous marble room and by
unspoken agreement proceeded down the stairs.
They were not steep, but his hand reached out,
pressing into the small of her back in a small
gesture of support.

It was meaningless. Absolutely nothing—yet
it was the sort of thing that would never have
been allowed to happen if he knew who she
was. The Royal Princess of Taquul could never
be simply touched by a commoner! But no one

knew her identity except the few servants who'd helped her get ready. She moved down the steps and unconsciously her body shifted with each step so that they were pressed together at the side, touching in a way that sent arrows of heat darting through her body.

At the bottom of the stairs, he gestured to the edge of the pool. 'Stand with me a while.' He said it like a command and she suppressed a smile. People didn't dare speak to her like that in Taquul—or anywhere.

She nodded her agreement. Not because he'd commanded her to do so but because there was nowhere else she wanted to be. His hand stayed pressed to her back, guiding her to the edge of the pool. There was a tall table they could have stood at, with ballerina waitresses circulating deftly through the crowds. It was everything they needed, so Johara wasn't sure why she found herself saying, 'Would you like to see something special?'

He turned to face her, his eyes narrowing in assessment before he moved his head in one short nod of agreement.

Relief burst through her. It should have signalled danger, but she was incapable of feeling anything except adrenalin. No, that wasn't true. She felt excitement too, and in the pit of her stomach, spinning non-stop, she also felt a burst of desire.

The man strode beside her, completely relaxed, his natural authority impossible to miss. She wondered if he was a delegate from a foreign country, or perhaps one of the powerful industry leaders often included in palace occasions. A wealthy investor in the country's infrastructure? He certainly moved with that indefinable air of wealth and power.

Steps led away from the pool—these older and less finessed than the marble—giving way to a sweeping path. She walked down it, and his hand stayed at the small of her back the whole way, spreading warmth through her body, turning her breath to fire inside her and deep in the pit of her stomach she had the strangest sense of destiny, as though something about him, this night, her choice to walk with him had been written in the stars a long, long time ago.

He couldn't have said why he was walking with her. From the moment he'd seen her across the crowded ballroom he'd felt a lash of something like urgency; a *need* to speak to her. The room had been filled with beautiful women in stunning couture, dripping in gemstones with ornate face masks. While her black gown clung to her body like a second skin, showcasing her generous curves to perfection, it had been a long time since Amir had allowed physical attraction to control his responses.

Desire wasn't enough.

So why was he allowing her to lead him away from the party—knowing he had to stand beside Sheikh Malik Qadir within the hour and showcase their newly formed 'friendship'? At least, for the sake of those in attendance, they had to pretend.

Nothing had changed for Amir though. He still hated the Qadirs with a passion. Nineteen years ago, with the death of his parents, he had sworn he would always hate them, and he intended to keep that promise.

'Where are you taking me?'

'Patience. We're almost there.' She spoke with a slight American accent and her voice was smooth and melodious, almost musical.

'Are you in the habit of taking men you don't know into the wilderness?'

She laughed, the sound as delicate as a bell. 'First of all, this is hardly a wilderness. The gardens are immaculately tended here, don't you think?'

He dipped his head in silent concession.

'And as for dragging men I don't know anywhere…' She paused mid-sentence, and stopped walking as well, her eyes latching to his in a way

that communicated so much more than words
ever could. He felt the pulse of response from
her to him, the rushing of need. Her breathing
was laboured, each exhalation audible in the
quiet night air. Overhead, the stars shone against
the desert sky, silver against velvet black, but
there was no one and nothing more brilliant
than the woman before him. His hands lifted to
her mask; he needed to see her face. He wanted
to see all of her. But her hands caught his, stilling them, and she shook her head a little.

'No. I like it like this.'

It was a strange thing to say—as though she
liked the anonymity the mask provided. He
dropped his hands lower, but instead of bringing them to his side he placed them at hers. His
touch was light at first, as though asking a question. In response, she swayed forward a little,
so her body brushed his and he was no longer
able to deny the onslaught of needs that were
assaulting him. He felt like a teenager again,
driven by hormones and lust. How long had it
been since he'd allowed himself to act on something so base?

'Come with me,' she murmured, hunger in
the words, desperation in the speed with which
she spoke. She reached down and grabbed his
hand, linking her fingers through his, pulling
him beside her. The night was dark and here

they were far from the revellers, but as an enormous shrub came out of nowhere he was grateful for the privacy it created. She reached for the loose branches and brushed them aside, offering him a mysterious look over her shoulder before disappearing through a wall made of trees. Her hand continued to hold his, but he stood on the other side a moment, looking in one direction and then another before stepping forward. Large, fragrant trees surrounded them, the foliage thick to the ground.

The sky overhead was the only recognisable feature, but even that was unable to cast sufficient light over the structure. It was black inside, almost completely, a sliver of moonlight offering the faintest silver glow.

'This way.' She pulled him a little deeper, her other hand on the leaves as if by memory, turning a corner and then another, and as they turned once more he could hear water, faint at first but becoming louder with each step. She didn't stop until they reached a fountain in the centre of this garden, this maze.

'It's beautiful, isn't it?' she asked, turning to face him. He didn't spare a glance for the space in which they stood. He was certain she was right, but he couldn't look away from her. He ached to remove her mask; even if he did so, he would barely be able to see her face, given how dark it was this deep in the maze.

'Yes.' The word was guttural and deep.

He lifted a hand to her chin, taking it between his thumb and forefinger and holding her steady, scrutinising her as though if he looked hard enough and long enough he could make sense of this incredible attraction.

'It's famous, you know. The Palace Maze.'

He nodded. 'I've heard of it.'

'Of course. Everyone in Taquul has.' She smiled, a flash of dark red lips. He didn't correct her; she didn't need to know he was from Ishkana—nor that he was the Sheikh of that country.

He continued to stare at her and her lips parted, her eyes sweeping shut so beyond the veil of her mask he could see two crescent-shaped sets of lashes, long and thick.

He should leave. This wasn't appropriate. But leaving was anathema to him; it was as though he were standing in quicksand, completely in her thrall.

'How long are you in Taquul for?'

Something shifted in her expression, in the little he could see of it, anyway. 'I don't know.'

'You don't like it here?'

She expelled a soft sigh. 'I have mixed feelings.'

It made more sense than such a vague statement should have. 'What do you do in New York?'

Her smile now was natural. 'I started the Early Intervention Literacy Association. I work on childhood literacy initiatives, particularly for children aged four to seven.'

It surprised him; he hadn't been expecting her to say anything like that. She looked every inch the socialite, the heiress, rather than someone who rolled up her sleeves and worked on something so important.

'What drew you to that?'

Her eyes shuttered him out even as she continued to look at him, as though there was something she wanted to keep secret, to keep from him. He instantly hated that. 'It's a worthwhile cause.'

He wanted to challenge her, to dig deeper, but he felt he was already balancing on a precipice, and that the more he knew was somehow dangerous.

'Yes.' Silence wrapped around them, but it was a silence that spoke volumes. His dark eyes bore into hers—a lighter shade of brown, like oak, sunshine and sand. He stared at her for as long as he could before dropping his eyes to her lips, then lower still to the curve of her breasts. The dress was black but so glossy it shimmered in the gentle moonlight.

'This is incredible,' he muttered, shaking his head as he ran his hand along her side, his fingertips brushing the flesh at her hips, then higher, tantalising the sweet spot beneath her arms, so close to her breasts he could see her awareness and desire, the plea in her eyes begging him to touch her there. His arousal hardened; he wanted to make love to her right here, beneath the stars, with the trees as their witness to whatever this madness was.

'How long are you in Taquul for?'

Only as long as he absolutely needed to be.

Every moment in this kingdom felt like a betrayal to his parents and their memory. 'Just this event. I leave immediately afterwards.'

Her eyes glittered with something like determination and she nodded. 'Good.' It was a purr. A noise that was half invitation, half dare. The latter made no sense but the former was an utter relief.

'In answer to your earlier question, I don't ever do this.'

He was quiet, waiting for her to say something else, to explain.

'I don't ever drag men I don't know into the maze, or anywhere.'

Her breath snagged in her throat, her lips parted and her head tilted back, her eyes holding his even as she swayed forward, totally surrendering to the madness of this moment.

'But you're different.'

His smile was barely a shift of his lips.

'Am I?'

'For starters, you're the only man here wearing black robes.'

He nodded slowly. There was a reason for that. Robes just like these had been worn at an ancient meeting between these two people, an event to mark their peace and friendship. His choice of attire was ceremonial but yes, she was right. All the other men wore either western-style suits or traditional white robes.

'Except, it's not what you're wearing.'

She lifted a hand, pressing her fingers to his chest. The touch surprised them both, but she didn't pull away.

'Have you ever met someone and felt…?' She frowned, searching for the right word.

But it was unnecessary. She didn't need to explain further. He shook his head. 'No. I've never felt this in my life.'

And before either of them could say another word, he dropped his mouth to hers and claimed her lips with all the desire that was humming inside his body.

CHAPTER TWO

THE DRESS WAS impossibly soft and, at its back, small pearls ran the length of her spine, so he had to undo each one in order to free her from the stunning creation. He was impatient and wanted to rip the dress—but the material was seemingly unbreakable. Besides, he had just enough sense left to realise he'd be doing this woman a great wrong if he left her to emerge from the maze with a snagged dress.

What they were doing was mad on every level. He knew nothing about her—he could only be grateful she knew nothing about him either. The last thing he needed was a complication that would detract from the peace accord.

She'd been right about the masks. Anonymity was perfect. He removed the dress as quickly as he could, stripping it from her body with reverence, a husky groan impossible to contain when he saw the underwear she wore. Flimsy white lace, it barely covered her generous breasts and bottom. The effect of the silk and her face mask had his cock growing so hard it was painful.

He swore under his breath, dispensing with his own robes with far less reverence, stripping out of them as he'd done hundreds of time before, unable to take his eyes off her as he moved. He was half afraid she'd change her mind, that she'd tell him they had to stop this. And she'd be right to do so! This was utter madness, a whim of desire and pleasure and hedonism, a whim he should deny himself, just as he'd denied himself so many things in his time for the sake of his country.

He knew that his kingdom required him to marry—he was the sole heir to the throne and without a wife the necessary children were impossible to beget. Yet he had only ever engaged in careful, meaningless affairs, and only when he'd felt the conditions were right—the right woman, who would understand he could give her nothing in the way of commitment, because he had an obligation to marry for the good of his kingdom. Did this woman understand that?

She reached around behind her back, as if to unclasp her bra, drawing his mind away from his thoughts and back to the present. He watched as she unhooked the lace, her breath hissing between her teeth, her eyes on his as the garment dropped to the ground beside her, revealing two perfect, pale orbs with dark, engorged nipples.

He swore again, and when her eyes dropped to his very visible arousal, he felt a little of his seed spill from his crown. Her eyes looked as though they wanted to devour him.

Aljahim, he wanted this. He wanted to feel her, to taste her, to touch her all over, but time was against them. This would be so much faster than he wanted.

'I cannot stay long,' he said quietly; it was only fair to forewarn her of that before they began.

'Nor can I.' She reached for the elastic of her tiny scrap of underwear but he shook his head.

'Allow me.'

Her eyes widened and she dropped her hands to the side, nodding once.

He closed the distance between them, pausing right in front of her, his pulse slamming through his body.

'This is what you want?'

She nodded.

'You're on the pill?'

Another nod, wide-eyed, as though the reality was just dawning on her.

'I don't have any protection—'

'I'm safe.'

He nodded. 'As am I.'

She bit down on her lip, a perfect cherry red against the dark hue of her skin. He ached to remove the mask and see her face, and yet it also served to draw attention to her lips and eyes, both of which were so incredibly distracting.

'Please.'

The single word was his undoing. He groaned, kissing her once more, dragging her lower lip into his mouth and moving his tongue so that it duelled with hers, teasing her at first before dominating her completely, so her head dropped backwards in surrender and he pillaged her mouth, each movement designed to demand compliance—yet it was he that was complying too, with the current of need firing between them a most superior force.

His hands cupped her naked breasts, feeling their weight, their roundedness, pushing his arousal forward against the silk of her underpants so she whimpered with need—a need he understood.

Her fingers dug into his shoulders, her body weak against his. He understood. It was overwhelming. He broke the kiss simply so he could drag his mouth lower, over her décolletage, conscious of the way his facial hair left marks as he went, his teeth adding nips, something primal and ancient firing inside him at the sight of his proof of possession. If he were less fired by desire he might have felt ashamed by such an ancient thrill, but he didn't.

He took one of her ample breasts into his mouth, seeking her nipple with his tongue, rolling the sweet flesh until she was whimpering loudly into the night sky. Only then did he transfer his attention to the other breast, lifting his thumb and forefinger to continue the pleasurable torment on the other. She bucked her hips forward; he knew how she was feeling, for his own body was racked with the same sense of desperation.

He wanted her but he didn't want to stop this yet. He could feel her pleasure tightening, her body responding to his instantly, and he wanted to indulge that responsiveness, to show her how perfectly they were suited. With his teeth clamping down against her nipple and his fingers teasing the other, he wedged her legs apart with his knee then brought his spare hand to rest there, parting the elastic from her with ease to allow a finger to slide into her warm, feminine core.

She groaned, a sound of complete pleasure and surrender and delight. He didn't stop. He pushed another finger into her depths and then used his thumb to stroke her, pleasuring her breasts as he paid homage to her.

She crumpled against him; his arms, his mouth, were holding her body in place. He felt her stiffen then, and begin to shake; she was exploding, gripping him hard as her body was racked with an intense, blinding release. He didn't relinquish his touch; he held her close, the squeezing of her muscles against his fingers eliciting an answering response from him.

He needed her; there was nothing else for it. Before her breath could calm he let her go, moving his hands to her hips instead, holding her steady as he knelt in front of her. His teeth caught the elastic of her underpants, pulling them loose and lower, low enough for her to step out of, and then he kissed her feminine core, his tongue flicking her until she was crying again, moaning, and, for lack of a name, she could only say 'please', again, and again, and again.

He smiled against her. Yes, he'd give her what she wanted—and what he wanted—and he'd do it soon. He stood, scooping her up and kissing her lips, unspeakably aroused by the idea that she might taste herself in his kiss, carrying her to a soft patch of grass to the right of the fountain. He laid her down, then took a moment to simply marvel at the view she made. Her body was curvy and slim all at once, her hair dark and tumbled around her shoulders, her mask adding an element of mystery and allure—not that she needed it.

This woman was the definition of alluring—distracting and perfect. What other explanation could there be for the instant attraction he'd felt for her? It was as though the very heavens had demanded this of him—of them. This was so out of character and yet it didn't feel wrong.

He brought his body over hers, feeling her softness beneath the hard planes of his frame, his mouth seeking to reassure her with kisses as his knee parted her legs, making way for him. He hovered at her entrance, the moment one he wanted to frame in time, caught like one of the butterflies he'd chased as a child and occasionally held in the palms of his hand for a precious instant before releasing it back into the forest. He caught her wrists in his, pinning them above her head, holding her still, and as he pushed up to watch her face as he entered her, he committed every instant of their coming together to his memory. Her eyes widened before sweeping shut as her lips parted on a husky moan, her hips lifting instinctively to welcome him to her body.

She was so tight, her muscles squeezing him almost painfully, so he moved more slowly than his instincts wanted, taking her bit by bit until he was buried inside then pausing, allowing her to grow used to this feeling before he moved, pulling back a little then driving forward, his hips moving slowly and then, as her cries grew more fervent, taking her harder, faster. His grip on her wrists loosened, his fingers moving instead to entwine with hers, squeezing her hands before releasing her so she wrapped her arms around his back, her nails scoring his flesh with each thrust. Her cries grew louder and her muscles tightened then fell into spasm and he felt the moment she lost her grip on reality and tumbled off the side of the world in an intense orgasm. She writhed beneath him and a moment later he joined her in that ecstasy, allowing his body the total surrender to hers and this moment, releasing himself to her with a hoarse cry that filled the heart of this maze with their pleasure.

She should have felt regret but she couldn't. She watched as he dressed, covering his body with the black robes—a body that she had somehow committed to memory. It was a honed frame, all muscle and strength, and on his left pectoral muscle, he had words tattooed in Latin in a cursive font: *amor fati*. His back bore signs of her passion all over it. Her fingernails had marked his smooth, bronzed skin, leaving a maze of their own in bright red lines, frantic and energised. A smile played about her lips, her body still naked beneath the glorious night sky, the sound of the water fountain adding an air of magic to what they'd just done. Or perhaps it wasn't the fountain, it was just the act.

Pleasure exploded through her. Relief. As though what she'd done was a connection to her true self, a timely reminder that she was an autonomous being, not controlled by this kingdom and her brother, by the expectations upon her. And it was more than that—it was as though the heavens themselves had conspired to bring them together. It had all happened so quickly, so completely, his possession of her so absolute. She'd only been with one other man before, Matthew, and she'd thought herself to be in love with him. She'd presumed that was a prerequisite to enjoying sex.

Enjoying sex!

What a bland way to express what she'd just felt! Her soul had changed orientation. North was now south, the world had altered shape, everything was different. She hadn't known what her body was capable of until a master such as this man had taught her how to truly feel. Wonderment filled her.

She knew only one regret then—that this wasn't the beginning of something more. It was impossible to hope for that. She wasn't utterly deluded as to her position in the royal family to think she could shun her obligations so completely and pursue a sexual fling with some random man—even one of obvious wealth and importance.

A sigh left her lips; she reached for a blade of grass, the dew on its tip delicate and glistening in the moonlight. The man turned to face her, and she smiled at him as though it were the most natural thing in the world. He smiled back; there were no barriers between them.

'Let me help you.' His voice was deep and husky, tinged with a slight accent. She couldn't quite pick it. She'd presumed he was from Taquul but perhaps he was from a neighbouring state, here to mark the new peace in the region.

Her brain was beginning to work again, after the fog of desire had made thinking impossible. He reached for her underwear, holding it out to her, the smile still on his face so something shifted in the pit of her stomach. He was so handsome, but it was more than that. She'd met plenty of handsome men before, and never felt like this. Powerful men, too. Handsome, strong, wealthy, sophisticated. After Matthew, she'd been difficult to impress. *Once bitten, twice shy* had become somewhat of a mantra for Johara without her realising it.

Perhaps it came down to the fact she knew nothing about him—he hadn't lied to her, he couldn't have, because they hadn't spoken. They'd let their bodies and mutual desire do all the communicating. Pleasure had been paramount.

Her nipples tingled as she slipped the bra into place, and he expelled a harsh breath as her underpants covered her femininity, so she knew he too regretted the necessity of ending this. Beyond the walls of this maze a party raged, a party at which she was expected to stand at her brother's side. Soon, the masks would come off, for the members of royal family at least, so that they could stand before the Sheikh of Ishkana as their true selves, and see his true self, pledging a better future for their two countries. And just for a moment, a blade of something like worry punctured the perfection of this moment. She pushed it away; she couldn't let it ruin this wonderful thing she'd just done.

Yet she had always hated everything the Haddad family was—that hate had been taught to her from a young age and even now, as a twenty-five-year-old woman, when she could acknowledge it was an ancient prejudice she'd been brought up to bear, she couldn't free herself from those feelings.

The idea of standing beside Malik and pretending she welcomed the Sheikh of Ishkana filled her with abhorrence. But she must do it. This encounter had been her act of rebellion, a

last, secret giving-in to her own needs. Now she
must be what her country needed.

'This dress is unlike anything I've ever seen.'
He ran his fingers over it then held it open for
her to step into. She moved closer, lifting one
foot and placing it in the middle of the dress,
putting a hand on his shoulder to steady herself. She'd marked him there too; little finger-
nail crescents were woven over his skin like a
pattern that told of her impatience and need.
She stroked the marks absent-mindedly as she
moved her other foot into the dress.

'It's made of spider silk.'

The jerk of his head towards hers showed
surprise.

'It was my mother's,' she added. 'Made a long
time ago, and over the course of many years. A
tribe to the west spent a long time harvesting
the silk of spiders and spinning it using a special loom.' She ran her hands over it then turned,
so he could fasten the buttons at the back. 'It's
virtually unbreakable. It's supposed to signify
strength and courage.'

His hands stilled a little at the small of her
back before continuing with her buttons. 'Do
you need these things?'

She thought of what was ahead and nodded.
'We all do, don't we?'

He reached the top button and pressed it into

place, then let his hands move over her shoulders without answering. She turned to face him, looked up into his face and smiled.

'Thank you.' It was a strange thing to say but she felt gratitude. They'd never see each other again but what they'd just done had been incredibly important to her.

He dipped his head in silent concession. 'I have to go back.'

Her brow furrowed behind her mask as she looked to the entrance of the heart of the maze. 'Me too.'

He took her hand in his. 'Lead the way, *inti qamar.*'

My moon. She smiled at the casual term of endearment, pushing through the maze effortlessly.

'You know the way well.'

'Yes.' She could have elaborated on that. She could have said that she used to come here to hide as a child, that the maze was hers alone. The gardeners who tended it had brought her treats for the days when she would come with a book and lie on the grass for hours on end. Not the kind of food that was served in the palace, all perfect and delicate and with the expectation that she sit with her back ramrod straight and make polite conversation with the children her parents had deemed suitable companions. No, here in the maze she'd feasted on food from beyond the palace walls, street food and market delicacies that the gardeners had brought in for her. Sticky pastries, figs that were sun-dried and exploding with flavour, spiced meatballs, marinated cheese, rice stuffed into vegetables and packed with spices. It was messy and organic, each mouthful a tribute to life and goodness. She could have told him that in this maze she'd spent some of her happiest times—and that tonight had simply added to that.

But instead, she simply nodded, already feeling as though the woman who'd just done such a daring and spontaneous thing was disappearing, being pushed deep inside Johara. The closer they moved to the start of the maze, the more she was reminded of the life that was ahead of her.

Rebellion aside, she couldn't keep hiding in mazes for ever. She was a princess of Taquul and that brought with it obligations and expectations. She would do as her brother said. She would stand at his side tonight and welcome the peace accord and then, if he insisted on it, she would consider the marriage to Paris, even though the idea turned her blood to ice.

At the entrance to the maze, she paused, pulling her hand from his and rubbing her fingers together.

'You go ahead of me,' she said, simply. 'It's not worth the trouble of being seen coming out of the maze together.'

He seemed to consider that a moment and then nodded. She had no idea what else she could say.

'If things were different,' he murmured, lifting a hand to her chin, holding her steady beneath him, 'I would have liked to see you again.'

Her answering smile was lopsided with wistfulness. 'If things were different,' she agreed, 'I would have liked that too.'

Neither said what their commitments were and why it wasn't possible. They didn't need to.

'Goodnight.' He bowed his head low in a mark of deference and respect, something she was used to, so for a moment she wondered if perhaps he'd guessed at her identity. But, no. He was simply showing her what their assignation had meant to him; how he viewed her. Her heart felt as though it had exploded to three times its size. She kept a polite smile in place, used to maintaining an expression of polite calm when she felt anything but.

'Goodnight...sir.'

CHAPTER THREE

'GOODNIGHT, SIR.'

Her words hummed through his brain, flooding him with memories. His body felt as though it was infused with a special kind of energy. He emerged from the maze, stalking past the pool, deliberately evading anyone who might try to catch his eye. At the entrance to the ballroom though, he could no longer ignore his reason for coming to this place he'd always despised.

Ahmed, his long-time servant, stepped from the shadows. 'Your Highness.' He bowed low, and Amir stilled, pushing aside thoughts of the beautiful woman and what they'd just shared. The entire encounter had been like a dream and already the threads of it were drifting away, impossible to catch.

'It's time.'

Amir nodded once, scanning the ballroom. 'Where is he?'

'In the stateroom.'

Amir's eyes narrowed with determination. 'Take me there.'

'Yes, sir.'

Amir paused as her words filled his brain once more. He walked beside his servant, using every ounce of willpower not to look over his shoulder to see the woman return to the ball-room. He wouldn't look for her again; he couldn't.

At the doors to the stateroom, Ahmed said something low and quiet to one of the guards. Both bowed low then opened the doors inwards.

There were only three men in the room, though the space was opulent and large enough to house two hundred easily. Marble, like the ballroom, with pillars to the vaulted ceilings, and tapestries on the walls—burgundy and gold with threads of navy blue to add detail.

Amir strode through the room as though he belonged. These men had removed their masks; he identified Malik Qadir easily enough.

'Your Majesty.' Malik silenced the other two with the address, extending a hand to Amir's. Amir hesitated a moment, his veins pounding with hatred and enmity. Only a love for his kingdom had him lifting up to remove his own mask before taking the outstretched hand and meeting Malik's eyes.

'Your Majesty,' he returned. But it felt like a

betrayal of everything he knew in the world; he felt as though he was defacing the memory of his parents by treating this man—the nephew of his parents' murderer!—with such civility. He had always sworn to hate this family, and that included the Sheikh and Princess of Taquul.

'My chief aide, Tariq.' Malik indicated the man to his left. Amir nodded and introduced Ahmed with the same title.

'And Paris—my friend, and the man my sister is to marry.'

Amir nodded. He didn't say that it was a pleasure. He was honest to a fault and always had been. But he forced his lips into something approximating a smile. 'Let's get this over with, then.'

Malik's eyes glittered, showing a matching sense of antipathy. They were both putting aside their personal hatred for the sake of their kingdoms. For peace and prosperity and in the hope that more senseless deaths could be avoided.

'One moment,' Malik murmured, turning to Tariq and speaking low and soft. They shared the same language but he swapped to an ancient dialect that Amir only passingly understood.

A moment later, Malik looked at Amir. 'My sister is expected.'

Paris's smile was indulgent. 'She is often late.'

It was clear from Malik's expression that he

disapproved of that quality. It was a sentiment Amir shared. Punctuality was not difficult to master and was, at its base, a sign of respect.

'Would you care for some wine?' Malik gestured to the wall, where a tray had been placed with several drinks.

Amir shook his head.

'Then we shall simply wait.'

The silence was tense. It was not natural. To be in the depths of this palace, surrounded by men who a year ago might have wished him dead? Hell, who probably still did. The peace talks had been ongoing, difficult and driven by emotion on both sides. It had taken Amir and Malik's intervention with their aides to achieve what they had.

And now, there was simply this. To stand in front of the assembled guests and speak to the importance of what they hoped to achieve, the ancient bonds that had, at one time, held these countries together. The mountain ranges separated them but that had, generations ago, been a passage alive with trade. The cooler climates there had created villages full of people from both countries. Only in recent times had the mountain range come to serve as a barrier.

He must focus on their past, on the closeness that had once been natural to their peoples, and on the future they intended to forge.

* * *

'I know, I know.' Johara ran a hand over her hair, meeting her servant's eyes in the gold-framed mirror. 'I'm late.'

'Very,' Athena agreed, pursing her lips into a small smile. 'Your brother was expecting you in the staterooms fifteen minutes ago.'

Another flicker of rebellion dashed through her soul. So she was keeping her brother waiting. It was juvenile and silly, particularly given the importance of the evening, and yet there was pleasure in the perversity of running behind schedule.

'Send word that I'm on my way,' she murmured to another servant, reaching up to remove the thick black ribbons that held the mask in place. Her hair was loose; it tumbled over her shoulders, but for this meeting, she wanted it styled more severely, more formally. That felt like an armour she would need.

Her hands worked deftly, catching the lustrous brown waves low at her nape and swirling them into a bun. 'Pins?'

Athena reached into her pockets—from which she seemed capable of removing all sorts of implements at will—and handed several to Johara. 'I can call a stylist?'

'Is it necessary?' Johara returned archly,

pressing several pins into place to secure an elegant chignon.

'No. It's perfect. Neat and ordered.'

The opposite of how she presently felt. When she lifted her hands to her cheeks to pinch them for a hint of colour, her nipples strained against the lace of her bra and she felt a hum of memory, a reminder of what she'd shared with the stranger. A *frisson* ran the length of her spine—had it really happened? It was the most uncharacteristic thing she'd ever done in her life and yet she didn't regret it. Not even a little.

'Lipstick.' Athena passed a black tube over and Johara coloured her full lips and then nodded.

'Fine. Let's go.'

She didn't portray a hint of the turmoil she was feeling. Her country stood on a precipice. Everything was new. The old ways must be forgotten. He had been wrong to say hatred would persist. The possibility of peace and safety was too alluring. Surely their people would force themselves to forget the anger and bigotry and come to see the people of Ishkana as their brothers and sisters?

She was barely conscious of the way servants bowed to her as she walked. It hadn't been like this in New York but, despite the fact she'd lived there for several years, she had grown up here in Taquul, for the most part, and this sort of respect came part and parcel with her position.

At the doors of the stateroom, she paused, turning to Athena. 'You'll come with me.'

'Of course.' Athena's eyes dropped to the marble floor a moment, as though she too was fortifying herself for the night ahead. And that was natural—Athena had served the Taquul royal family since she was a teenager, her sentiments matched theirs.

Beyond that, she was a friend to Johara. Johara reached out and squeezed Athena's hand for comfort. 'Let's just get it over with.' She unknowingly echoed Amir's earlier sentiments. The doors swept open, the noise of their intrusion drawing the attention of all in the room.

Her eyes naturally gravitated towards her brother's. His gaze held a warning, as though he expected her to make trouble in some way. From him, she turned to Paris. His smile was kind; she returned it. She might not find him at all attractive but he was sweet and they'd been friends for a long time.

Someone moved at the side of the room, catching her attention. She turned that way naturally, and missed her step, stumbling a little awkwardly as her eyes tried to make sense of it.

The man across the room was...unmistakably...the same man she'd made love to in the heart of the maze. His dark robes were instantly recognisable, but it was more than that. Though he'd worn a mask his face was...she'd seen it as they'd kissed. She'd *known* what he looked like.

Had he known who she was? Had it been some kind of vile revenge?

No. Shock registered on his features too, though he covered that response much more swiftly than she was able, assuming a mask of cool civility while her blood was threatening to burn her body to pieces.

'Jo.' Malik crossed to her but she couldn't look away from Amir. She saw the way he flinched at her name and wondered why. The world was spinning, and not in a good way. Malik put his hand under her elbow, guiding her deeper into the room, and she was glad for his support. She could hardly breathe. What were the chances?

He *had* to have known. He had come to speak to her out of nowhere—why else had he approached her like that? It couldn't have been random happenstance.

Except he hadn't known; she was sure of it. They'd both sought anonymity. It had been a transaction between two people: faceless, nationless, without identity. It had been about him and her, their bodies and souls, and nothing more.

She dropped her head, almost unable to walk

for a moment as the reality of what had happened unravelled inside her.

He'd use this to destroy her. To destroy her brother. If Malik knew what she'd done... Oh, heck.

Panic seized her.

'Calm down,' Malik muttered from the side of his lips. 'This is to commemorate a peace treaty, remember? He is no longer the enemy yet you look as though you would like to kill him.'

Startled, she jerked her eyes away from Sheikh Amir of Ishkana and looked at her brother instead. 'I would.'

Malik's expression showed amusement and then he shook his head, leaned closer and whispered, 'Me too, but my advisors tell me it would be a bad idea.'

She forced a smile she didn't feel. Paris moved to them, putting a familiar hand on hers and pressing a kiss to her cheek. It was a simple greeting, one that was appropriate for old friends, but in front of Amir, after what they'd just shared, she felt as though she should distance herself. She needed space. From him, from everyone. But it wasn't possible. There were far greater concerns than her personal life.

'Amir.' Malik addressed him by his first name, and it didn't occur to Amir to mind. In that moment, all of his brain power was absorbed in making sense of what the hell had just happened.

She was… Johara? The Princess of Taquul? The woman he'd made love to, been so blindsided by that he'd given into physical temptation against all common sense was…a Qadir?

He wanted to shout: *It can't be!* Surely it wasn't possible. And yet…there was no refuting it. Her dress…she moved and he remembered how she'd felt in his hands, how her body had writhed beneath his. He could close his eyes and picture her naked, her voluptuous curves calling to him, even as she now walked elegantly towards him, her hair neat, her make-up flawless, and he saw only a Qadir princess. Her parents had hated his. Her uncle Johar had killed his parents. Johar… Johara. She'd been named for that murderous son of a bitch.

Something like nausea burst through him. Hatred bubbled beneath his skin. As she came close, he inhaled and caught a hint of her fragrance, so familiar to him that his body couldn't help but respond, despite the fact he now knew who she was.

'This is my younger sister, Princess Johara of Taquul.'

Their eyes met and locked. It was impossible to look away. He saw fear there. Panic. But why? Because of what they'd done? Or because of what she thought he might do next? Did she believe he was going to announce their prior relationship? That he'd do something so foolish as confess what they'd shared? To what end?

His eyes narrowed imperceptibly and he extended a hand. 'A pleasure to meet you.'

He saw the moment relief lit her eyes. Her smile was barely there—a terrible facsimile of the vibrant smiles she'd offered in the maze. She hadn't known who he was. Neither of them had understood.

How had he failed to notice the signs though? Her familiarity with the maze. A dress made of spiders' silk. Both such obvious signs of her place within this family. Yet he'd been blinded by her, and by the attraction he felt. It was the only answer.

'Likewise.' Her accent. It was so American— naturally he'd assumed she was a foreigner, here in Taquul just for the ball. But now he recalled the biographical details he'd been furnished with prior to this treaty: that her mother had been American, that she'd gone to school in America for some time, and had lived there for several years.

'You look flushed. Do you feel well?' It was Paris, to her left. Something else flared in Amir's mind.

The man my sister is to marry.

'I'm fine.' At least she had the grace to look ashamed.

'Your Highness? They're ready.'

It was a blur. Johara stood between her brother and Paris as the peace accord was announced. Fireworks burst overhead to celebrate the occasion, and answering displays were seen across the countries. Peace had come—she could only hope that it would hold.

And all the while, those in attendance smiled and nodded with rapt faces, and finally cheered, so Johara smiled along with them and nodded as her brother spoke. But it was when Amir began to address the crowd that everything inside her dissolved into a kind of never-ending tumult.

'For too long we have seen our people die. We have fought over nothing more significant than on which side of the mountains we were born; this war has been a plague on both our countries. Our people were once unified and great, strong in this region, capable of anything. Our prosperity was shared, our might universally known. It is time to set aside the last one hundred years. It is time to forge a peace between our people, a lasting peace—not into the next century, but the next millenium.' She was captivated, staring at his deep, dark eyes as he scanned the crowd.

'It will take work. It will require us to actively forget how we have been taught to feel. We will need to look behind the masks of what we believe our peoples stand for, to see the truth of what is there. A baker in Ishkana is no different from a baker in Taquul. We see the same stars, worship the same god, dance to the same songs, have learned all the same tales. We can be unified once more.' He turned to look at Malik, but his eyes glanced over Johara, so she was sure he must have seen the effect his rousing speech had on her.

She couldn't hide her admiration, she was sure of it.

'Tonight begins a new way of life for us, a life of peace.'

Silence lasted for several seconds and then applause broke out, loud and joyous. If Johara had been in any doubt as to how desperately the people wished for peace, the proof was right before her now. And for Amir to take what was largely a crowd of Taquul dignitaries and have them eating out of his hand—it showed the magnetism he had.

Not that she needed any further indication of that.

The official requirements of the evening were

at an end. She left the makeshift stage gratefully, giving a brief farewell to Paris before slipping through thick gold curtains that hung along
the edge of the ballroom. She moved quickly,
desperately needing air, space, a way to breathe.
She found her way to a long marble corridor
and moved through it until she reached glass
doors at the end.

The cool desert air glanced across her skin as
she pushed them open, onto a small Juliet balcony that overlooked the Sheikh's aviary, where
his prized falcons were kept. In the evening, the
stark outline of trees was striking. Beyond it,
the desert lay, and the light breeze stirred the
sand, so when she breathed in she could smell
that acrid clay that was so reminiscent of her
childhood. How she'd loved to carry bottles of
water into the desert and pour it over the sand
to make little streams, turning the sand into a
malleable substance from which she could build
great structures.

For a child who could barely read, making
things with her hands had been her own source
of satisfaction.

'Your Highness.'

She stiffened, curving her hands over the railing of the balcony as his voice reached her ears.
Had she known he would follow? No. And yet,
she was hardly surprised.

She turned slowly, bracing for this—or at least attempting to. Nothing could prepare her for what was to come. Without his mask, alone on the balcony, so close she could touch him. And more than that, the coldness in his face. The anger. Oh, he was trying to control it but she felt it emanating from him in waves so she rushed to say, 'I didn't know who you were. I had no idea.'

She knew, even as she spoke the words, that it wasn't completely true. Their connection had defied logic and sense. Perhaps she might have been able to resist him, but not if he'd set his mind on seducing her.

'So you simply took the chance to sleep with another man behind your fiancé's back?'

'I...' She frowned. 'I don't have a fiancé.'

That surprised him.

'There is a man my brother wishes me to marry,' she stressed, 'but that's not quite the same thing. Last time I checked, I still have some say in the matter, so no, I didn't "cheat" on anyone.'

He dipped his head forward. 'I apologise. I was misinformed.'

She was surprised by the instant apology, and more so how he could deliver it in a way that was both genuine and infused with icy coldness. If she turned to the right, she'd see the edge of the maze. She couldn't look that way. She'd likely never look at it again, certainly never walk within its verdant walls.

'You're named for him.'

She frowned, but only for a second. She should have remembered sooner, the awful, bloody death in her family's—and his family's—history. 'My uncle Johar? Yes.'

'You're named as a tribute.'

'I was born before he...'

Amir's shoulders squared. 'Murdered my parents?'

Her eyes swept shut in anguish. 'Yes.'

'And yet he had knowingly hated them for a long time.'

'You said yourself, hate has been felt by all our people for a very long time.'

'True.' He crossed his arms over his broad chest. She wished he hadn't done that. It drew her focus in a way that was dangerous, flooding her body and brain with too many feelings.

'A moment ago, I listened to you implore us to move on from those feelings. To remember that we were once allies.' She swallowed, not realising until that instant how badly she wanted that to be the case. 'Let's not speak of Johar. Not when a new period of peace is upon us.'

His lips curled into what she could only describe as a grimace of derision. 'Publicly I must advocate and encourage peace. Privately I am allowed to feel whatever the damned hell I please.'

His anger and vehemence were palpable forces, rushing towards her. 'And what do you feel?'

He stared at her for several seconds and then looked beyond her, beyond the aviary, to the desert planes in the distance, made silver by the moonlight. 'It's better not to discuss it with you.'

'If you'd known who I was…' She let the question hang between them unfinished.

'Would I have allowed it to happen?' He compressed his lips. 'No.'

'You think you could have stopped it?'

His eyes shifted back to hers and she saw it—what she'd been conscious of and yet not fully understood before. He was a king. Born all-powerful to a mighty people. Born to rule and fully cognisant of what the world required of him. His natural authority was exactly that. She'd perceived it from the outset and she felt it now. She shivered involuntarily, a whisper of cold seizing her core.

'Absolutely.'

Courage was failing her, but she wouldn't allow what they'd shared to be lost completely. 'You're wrong.' She moved forward, putting a hand on his chest, but he flinched away from her, his eyes holding a warning. Pain lashed her.

She had to be brave; he couldn't deny that what had happened between them was real. That it held meaning. 'There was something about you, and me, that needed us to do that.'

He made a noise of disagreement. 'It was a mistake.'

Hurt pounded her insides. She shook her head in disagreement.

'Let me be clear.' His voice was deep and authoritative. She stayed where she was, but her body was reverberating with a need to reach for him, to touch him. 'If I had known you were a Qadir I would not have touched you. I would not have spoken to you. I will always regret what happened between us, Johara.' And her spat her name as though it were the worst insult he could conjure. 'Tonight, I betrayed myself, my parents, and everything I have always believed.'

Pain exploded in her chest. She blinked at him, uncertain of how to respond, surprised by how badly his words had cut her. 'I'm not my uncle. I'm not my parents and I'm not my brother.' She spoke with a quiet dignity, her voice only shaking a little. 'You cannot seriously mean to hate me just because of the family I was born into?'

His eyes pierced her. 'I'm afraid that's exactly what I mean, Your Highness.'

CHAPTER FOUR

'IT'S IMPORTANT.'

'It's dangerous.' Paris spoke over Malik in a rare sign of anger. Johara watched the two of them discussing her fate with an overarching sense of frustration. As though where she went and why came down to what they said.

'The peace is already fraying, and only eight weeks after the accord was signed. We need to do something more to underscore our intent that this be meaningful.' He turned to Johara, frowning. 'I hate to ask it of you, Johara, but you know that it's time.'

She said nothing, simply lifting a brow in a silent invitation for him to continue. 'You've avoided your obligations for years, and I've allowed it.' Inwardly she bristled. Malik crouched before her. 'Because you're my sister and I love you; I want you to be happy. But I *need* you now. Someone has to go and do the sorts of visible politicking I don't have time for.'

She ignored the way her brother so easily relegated the responsibilities he was trying to foist on her as though it were just glad-handing and smiling for cameras, rather than wading into enemy territory and attempting to win the hearts of the Ishkana people.

'You should go.' Paris spoke quietly, addressing Malik, his eyes intense. 'For a short visit.'

'It's not possible.' Malik sighed. 'You know there are matters here that require my urgent attention.'

Paris expelled a breath. 'Then send someone. A diplomat. A cousin.'

'No. It can't be a snub, nor a regular visit. This has to have meaning to his people, the way his visit did for ours.'

'It can't have meant that much,' Paris pointed out, 'for the skirmishes to be continuing.'

'Sheikh Amir is right. We have to be unified in this.' Johara spoke above both of them, standing with innate elegance and striding towards one of the windows that framed a view of the citrus gardens. Their formal layout was designed as a tribute to a French palace, each tree surrounded by bursts of lavender, white gravel demarcating the various plantings.

Paris and Malik were silent; waiting.

'I hate the idea of going to Ishkana.' She did, but not for reasons she could ever share with either man. She had tried to forget everything about Sheikh Amir and his hateful kingdom since they'd spoken on the balcony; to be sent there now as a guest of the palace? She trembled at the idea, and with outrage, nothing more!

'So don't go,' Paris murmured.

'I have to.' She turned to face him, her smile dismissive. He was a good friend but the more time she'd spent back in Taquul, the more certain she'd become that she could never marry him. There was no doubt in her mind that he had her brother's best interests at heart, and yet that wasn't enough. She would speak to him about it, put the idea from his mind once and for all. His concern was worrying because it suggested he cared for her in a way that went beyond duty to the Sheikh, and the last thing she wanted to do was hurt Paris.

'Malik is right. We have to show the people of Ishkana that we value this peace accord,' she said with quiet resolve. 'For our people, we must appear to be moving forward. We have to lead the way. How can we expect them to find peace in their hearts if we don't demonstrate it? I will go to Ishkana as a guest of the palace. I will attend state dinners and speak to the parliament. I will tour their ancient ruins and libraries and smile for the cameras. Is that what you want, Mal?'

He made a small noise of agreement. 'You know how I hate to ask it of you.'

She waved a hand through the air. 'If you hadn't asked, I would have suggested it. It's the best thing for everyone.'

'No, Johara. You will be exposed—'

'I'll be a guest of their King, will I not?'

Malik dipped his head forward in silent agreement.

'And staying in the palace?'

Another nod.

'So I presume His Majesty will vouch for my safety?'

'For what it's worth,' Paris responded dubiously.

At that, Malik held up a hand. 'I believe Amir is a man of honour.' The words were dark, troubled. 'He is a Haddad, so naturally I mistrust him, but I believe that, having invited you to the palace, he will go out of his way to ensure your safety.'

Johara's heart skipped a beat. 'Sheikh Amir invited me?'

Malik's smile was dismissive. 'A figure of speech. The suggestion came through diplomatic channels and no specific guest was mentioned. It was my idea that you should attend.'

'Of course.' She turned away again quickly, hoping she'd hid the look of disappointment she knew must be on her face. What had she expected? That he'd roll out the red carpet for her eight weeks after they'd last seen each other? He'd made his feelings perfectly clear that night.

It was a mistake. Her heart skipped another beat. It wasn't a mistake. It was the single greatest moment of her life and she wouldn't let him take that away from her. Oh, she desperately wished that they weren't who they were—the Haddads and Qadirs had hated each other for too long to allow it to be forgotten. But in that moment, it had been too perfect so even now she struggled to care.

'So you'll go?'

What would it be like to enter his kingdom? His palace? She'd never been to Ishkana. It wouldn't have been safe until recently. She'd seen photographs and knew much of its history, but to see it for herself? Curiosity sparked inside her, and she told herself the rushing of her pulse was owing to that alone.

'Yes, Mal. I'll go to Ishkana.'

In many ways, it was just like Taquul. The sand was the same colour, the heat was the same, the trees innately familiar. But as the limousine approached the palace she felt a flash of anticipation warm her skin. The approach to the palace was lined with palm trees, and on one side, a colourful market had been set up. The limousine was obliged to slow down as pedestrians meandered across the road, in no hurry to clear the way for the car. It gave her time to observe. An old woman sat in the shade cast from her brightly coloured market tent, an ancient spinning wheel before her. She moved effortlessly, each shift of the wheel an act she'd obviously repeated millions of times in her long lifetime. A vibrant red wool was being formed at one side. Another woman sat beside her, talking and cackling with laughter. The next stall showed spices, piled high in pyramids, just as vendors did at home, the next sold sweets—she recognised many of the same illicit delicacies she'd been introduced to by the gardening staff who'd tended the maze.

As the car neared the palace gates, she saw something that broke her heart. Several people stood in a cluster, shaded by a large, old umbrella. Their clothes were poor, their faces grubby and bodies frail. She turned to the driver, leaning forward. 'Stop the car.'

He pressed the brakes, looking over his shoulder. 'Madam?'

'A moment.' She spoke with all the authority she could conjure, unlocking her door and stepping out. The sun beat down on her relentlessly, causing a bead of perspiration to break out on her brow. She wiped at it but continued to walk to the group. There were perhaps eighteen people. She was conscious of one of the palace guards stepping out of the car and following behind her—she resented his intrusion, and the suggestion that these people must be dangerous because they happened to be poor.

Fixing him with a cool stare, she turned back to the people at the gate and smiled. 'It's warm,' she said to a woman in perhaps her early thirties, nursing an infant on her hip. The child looked at Johara with enormous brown eyes.

'Very hot, yes.'

'You need some lemonade from the markets,' Johara said with a smile. The mother's eyes widened but she shook her head almost instantly.

'It's not possible.'

'Here.' Johara reached into the folds of her linen dress, removing enough bank notes to pay rent for a month. She handed them to the mother, who shook her head.

'Please, take it. Buy some food and drink.' She gestured to the group behind her. 'For all of you.'

'But…it's very generous…'

Johara's heart turned over, and simultaneously she felt a blade of anger pierce her. How could Amir sit in his palace and allow this kind of poverty to exist on his doorstep? True, Taqul wasn't perfect but this was so blatant! So heart-wrenching.

'I insist.' She leaned out and tousled the little boy's hair. He didn't react at first but then he giggled, so Johara did it again.

'He likes you,' the woman said wistfully. 'It's the first time he's smiled in days.'

'I'm sorry to hear it,' Johara murmured truthfully. 'He has a beautiful smile.'

She turned to leave but before she'd gone three steps, the woman arrested her. 'What is your name, miss?'

Johara paused, aware that it was a turning point. She'd come to this country to spread word of the alliance and reverse people's opinions; now was as good a time to start as any.

'Johara Qadir,' she said without inflection— not anger, not cynicism, not apology.

A rippled murmur travelled the group but the woman spoke over it. 'Thank you, Your Highness.' And she bowed low, but with a smile on her face, so Johara was glad the people knew who she was.

The security guard followed her back to the car, and as he opened the door he said firmly, 'You should not have done that, madam.'

Johara's surprise was obvious. In Taquul, a servant would never speak to a guest in such a manner! 'I beg your pardon, why exactly not?'

'Because it is dangerous and the Sheikh gave your brother his word you would be safe here. That means he will want to control every aspect of your safety. If you display a tendency to make such poor decisions he'll likely confine you to the palace.'

She stared at him in disbelief. 'Confine me... *me*...to the palace?'

The guard lifted his shoulders. 'We should go. He will be waiting.'

Emotions flooded Johara's body. *He will be waiting.* The idea of Amir waiting for her did unreasonable things to her pulse.

She slid into the car, waving at her newfound friend as the car drove through the palace gates, trying to work out why her nerves wouldn't settle.

This wasn't about him. He'd made it very clear that he regretted what had happened between them and she had no choice but to accept that, to feel as he did.

Johara held her breath, marvelling at all the many ways in which the palace differed from the photographs she'd seen. Oh, it was enormous and impossibly grand, she knew parts of it had been constructed in the fifth century—the old stone foundations and underground tunnels and caverns rumoured to run all the way to the mountains—but the rest had been completed in the sixteen hundreds; enormous white stone walls with gold details formed an impressive façade. The windows were arched, the roofs shaped to match with colours of gold, turquoise and copper. Around the entire palace there was a moat of the most iridescent water, such a glorious pale blue it reminded her of the clearest seas of the Mediterranean.

She peered at it as they drove over the moat, then fixed her attention on the palace. The car stopped at a large golden door. Servants and guards stood to the ready and at the top of the stairs, him.

Amir.

His Majesty, Sheikh of Ishkana. Nerves fired through her but she refused to let them show, especially to the bossy security agent who'd told her she shouldn't have stopped to speak to the poor people at the gate. Since when was compassion forbidden?

The security agent opened the door without meeting her eyes and she stepped from the car, conscious of everything in that moment. Her dress, her hair, the fact *he* was staring at her and that everyone was watching them. Conscious of the photographer who stood poised to take an official photograph that would be printed in all the newspapers in both countries and around the world the following morning.

Most conscious of all though of Amir as he moved down the stairs towards her, his eyes not leaving her face, his face so familiar, so achingly familiar, that she could barely remember to act impassive.

It took all her self-control to stay where she was, a look of polite calm on her face. He extended a hand in greeting; she placed hers in it. The world stopped spinning all over again. Arrows drove through her skin. Her mouth was dry, breathing painful. She stared at him in bewilderment—she hadn't thought he'd still be able to affect her like that. She'd thought knowing who he was and how he felt about her might have changed…something.

She pulled her hand away as though he'd burned her, with no idea if the photographer had succeeded in capturing a suitably friendly photograph—and not particularly caring.

'Welcome, Princess,' he murmured, and, though it was a perfectly acceptable thing to say, she felt her skin crawl, as though he were condemning her title just as he had her name on that last night. 'Johara.' He'd spat it at her and she felt that again now.

'Thank you.' She didn't flinch.

'Smile for the camera,' he said quietly, leaning down so only she caught the words. She looked in the direction he'd nodded, eyeing off the photographer and lifting her lips in a practised smile. They stood there for a moment before the Sheikh put his hand to the small of her back, to guide her to the palace. It was too much. She wanted to jerk herself away from the simple contact, or she wanted to throw herself at his feet and beg him to do so much more.

She did neither.

Her upbringing and training kicked in; she put one foot in front of the other until she reached the top of the steps and then beyond them, into the cool corridor of the palace. Then, and only then, when out of sight of photographers, did she casually step beyond his reach.

If he noticed, or cared, he didn't show it. 'How was your flight?'

Like you care. The acerbic rejoinder died on the tip of her tongue. This would never work if she went out of her way to spar with him. 'Fine. Easy.'

'Easier still when we can repair and reopen the mountain roads; the drive will take a matter of hours.'

Johara looked towards him. 'That's what you intend?'

He began to move deeper into the palace and she followed after him. 'Why not? There were always easy links between our people. It's only as a result of the conflict that these have been shut down.'

'And trade?' she prompted.

'Naturally.'

She nodded, considering this. 'Even as the peace seems so tenuous?'

'I expected it would.' He shrugged. 'Surely you didn't truly believe it would be smooth sailing simply because Malik and I signed an accord?'

Her brow furrowed as she considered that. 'I...had hoped.'

'Yes.' The word was delivered enigmatically. 'You had hoped.'

'You're still cynical about this?'

They reached a pair of thick, dark wood doors, at which four guards stood sentinel. He gestured for her to precede him. She did so, without looking where she was going, so when she stepped into the space she was completely unprepared for what awaited her. She drew in a sharp breath, wonderment filling her gaze. She hadn't been paying attention; it had felt as though they were moving deeper into the palace, yet this room was a sanctuary of green. A stream ran in front of them, covered by dark timber bridges. The walls were dark wood, but filled with greenery. Vines had tentacles that reached across everything. Johara reached out and ran her fingers over the velvety surface of one of the plants.

Amir watched Johara.

'What is this?' She turned to face him, a smile unknowingly lifting her lips. It was impossible to feel anything but uplifted in this room.

'A private hall, now just for my use. It's one of the oldest spaces in the palace.'

She nodded, looking upwards, where several openings showed views of the sky. She could only imagine how stunning it would be in the evening.

'I'd never heard of it. It's not in any of the information we have.' Her cheeks grew hot. 'The texts, I mean.'

He lifted a brow. 'You've been studying my country?'

'As children, my brother and I were taught much about Ishkana.'

'And how to hate us?'

Her eyes flashed. 'As you were taught to hate us.'

'A lesson that I never really understood until I was twelve years old.'

She stared at him blankly.

Amir moved deeper into the room. 'The age I was when my parents were assassinated.'

Her heart squeezed for the boy he'd been. She wanted to offer condolences, to tell him how sorry she was, but both sentiments seemed disingenuous, given the strained nature of their relationship. So instead, she said, 'That must have been very difficult.'

He didn't respond. His profile was autocratic, his features tight. Where was the man she'd made love to in the maze? It felt like such a long time ago. Then, she'd had no inhibitions, no barriers. To him she would have known exactly what to say, without second-guessing herself.

'This room is completely private—for my use only, and for those guests I choose to invite here with me.' He tilted a gaze at her. 'I'm sure you are aware of how difficult it is to have true privacy in a palace.'

'Yes,' she agreed, looking around. The more she looked, the more she saw and loved. In the far corner, an old rug had been spread, gold and burgundy in colour, and against it, sumptuous pillows were spread. 'Thank you for showing it to me.'

He turned to face her, his eyes glittering like onyx in his handsome face.

'I wanted to speak to you. Alone.'

Her body went into overdrive. Blood hummed just beneath her skin, her heart slammed into her ribs and her knees began to feel as though they were two distinct magnetic poles. She walked slowly and deliberately towards the centre of the room, where an enormous fiddle leaf fig was the centrepiece. 'Did you, Amir?'

Using his name felt like both a rebellion and a comfort. She didn't look at him to see his reaction.

'It's been two and a half months since the masquerade.'

She studied the detailed, intricate veins in the leaves of the fig tree, her eyes tracing their patterns, every fibre of her being focussing on not reacting visibly to his statement.

'So you would know by now.'

'Know?'

'If there were any consequences to that night.'

Consequences? Her brain was sluggish. The heat, and having seen him again, made her feel a thousand things and none of them was mentally acute, so it took a few seconds for his meaning to make sense. Her breath snagged in her throat as she contemplated what he meant—something which hadn't, until that moment, even occurred to her. 'You mean to ask if I'm pregnant?'

The room seemed to hush. The gentle vines no longer whispered, the water beneath them ceased to flow, even the sun overhead felt as though it grew dim.

'Are you?'

Something painful shifted in her belly. She swallowed past a lump in her throat, turning to face him slowly. 'And if I were, Amir?' This time, when she said his name, she was conscious of the way he reacted, heat simmering in his eyes.

'I will not speak in hypotheticals.'

It was so like him. She felt a ridiculous burst of anger at his refusal to enter into a 'what if?'. 'No, that's not fair. You asked the question, I'm entitled to ask mine back. What would you do if I were pregnant?'

His face became shuttered, impossible to read, unfamiliar and intimidating. 'What would you have me do?'

She should have expected that. 'No, I'm asking what you would *want* to do.'

'Are you hoping I'll say something romantic, Johara? Do you wish me to tell you that I would put aside our ancient feud and marry you, for the sake of our child's future?'

Her lips parted. The image he painted was painful and somehow impossible to ignore. She shook her head even when she wasn't sure what she felt or wanted.

'Even for the sake of our child, I would not marry you. I couldn't. As much as I hate your family, you deserve better than that.'

Curiosity barbed inside her. 'You think marriage to you would be a punishment?'

'Yes. For both of us.'

'Why, Amir?'

He moved closer, and she held her breath, waiting, wanting, needing. 'Because I would never forgive you, Johara.' It was just like the first time he'd said her name. An invocation, a curse, a whip lashing the air in the room and crashing finally against the base of her spine.

'For what? What exactly have I done that requires forgiveness?'

'It is not what you've done.'

'But who I am? Born to the Qadir royal family?'

The compression of his lips was all the confirmation she needed.

'And what we shared changes nothing?'

'What we shared was wrong. It should never have happened.'

'How can you say that when it felt so right?'

His eyes closed for a moment then lanced her with their intensity. 'It was just sex.'

She stared at him in surprise. It was such a crude thing to say, and so wrong. She hadn't expected it of him.

'You weren't a virgin. You knew what sex was about.'

Her eyes hurt. It took her a second to comprehend that it was the sting of tears. She blinked furiously, refusing to give in to such a childish response.

'So that night meant nothing to you?'

He stared at her without responding. Every second that stretched between them was like a fresh pain in her heart.

'I'm not here to discuss anything besides the possibility that you conceived our child.'

Her heart lurched. She couldn't help it—out of nowhere an image of what their baby might look like filled her eyes, all chubby with dark hair and fierce dark eyes. She turned away from him, everything wonky and unsteady.

'I'm not pregnant, Amir. You're off the hook completely.'

She heard his hiss of relief, a sharp exhalation, as though he hadn't been breathing properly until then. She wanted to hurt him back, to make him feel as she did, but she feared she wasn't properly armed. How could one hurt a stone wall? And whatever she'd perceived in him on the night of the masquerade, she could see now that he was impenetrable. All unfeeling and strong, unyielding and determined to stay that way.

'If that's all, I'd like to be shown to my suite now.'

CHAPTER FIVE

'It is called *albaqan raghif*,' he said quietly, his eyes on her as she fingered the delicate piece of bread, his words murmured so they breathed across her cheek. She resisted the impulse to lean closer. This was the first she'd seen of him since their discussion earlier that day. For most of the day, she'd been given a tour of the palace by a senior advisor, shown the ancient rooms—the library, the art galleries, the corridors lined with tapestries so like those that hung in the palaces of Taquul. Looking at them had filled her with both melancholy and hope. A sadness that two people so alike and with such a richly shared history could have been so combative for so long, and hope that their shared history would lay the foundations for a meaningful future peace.

Now, sitting at the head of the room with him, various government ministers in attendance, she concentrated on what she'd come here for—this was a state visit and she the representative of Taquul—how she felt about the man to her right was not important. 'We have something similar in Taquul.' She reached for a piece of the pecan bread and bit into it. She concentrated on the flavours and after she'd finished her mouthful said, 'Except ours generally has different spices. Nutmeg and cardamom.'

'My mother made it like that,' Amir said with obvious surprise.

She took another bite and smiled at him politely. 'This is very good too.'

His eyes narrowed. 'But you prefer it the way you're used to.'

'I didn't say that.'

Silence stretched between them, all the more noticeable for how much conversation was swirling around the room. The mood was, for the most part, festive. Some ministers had treated her with suspicion, a few even with open dislike, but generally, people had been welcoming. It saddened her to realise how right Amir had been—the peace would not come easily. Prejudices died hard.

'I'm sorry your brother sent you.'

She was surprised by the words. She squared her shoulders, careful not to react visibly. 'You'd prefer I hadn't come?'

He angled his face to hers. 'As I'm sure you would have wished to avoid it.'

'On the contrary—' she reached for her wine glass '—I relished the opportunity.'

His eyes held hers curiously.

'I've heard a lot about Ishkana. All my life, stories have been told of your people, your ways, your ancient cities. To be here now is an exercise in satisfying my curiosity.'

He lifted his brows. 'What are you curious about?'

'Oh, everything.' She sipped her wine. 'The ruins of *wasat*, the wall that spans the *sarieun sea*, the theatres in the capital.' She shook her head, a smile playing about her full red lips. 'I know there won't be a chance on this visit, but in time, with continued peace between our people, these landmarks could open up.'

He appeared to consider that for a moment. 'Yes. In time.'

'And our historical sites will be open to your people as well.'

He regarded her for several long moments, then sighed. 'You are an optimist.'

She laughed softly, spontaneously. 'Am I?'

Photographers were not permitted at royal banquets. It was a long-established protocol and even in this day of cell phones no cameras were used during meals. If anyone had taken a photo in that second though it would have captured two royals with their faces close together, their eyes latched, a look of something very like intimacy in their position. To a few of those present, the idea of the powerful, feared and adored Sheikh Amir Haddad sharing a meal with the Princess of Taquul was likely a bitter pill to swallow.

'If I am,' she murmured, after several seconds, 'then you must be too.'

His expression was unchanged. 'I don't think I've ever been accused of that.'

'It's not an accusation so much as an observation,' she corrected.

'Fine. That has never been...observed...of me before.'

'Doesn't it take a degree of optimism to proceed with a peace treaty? You must believe it will succeed or why bother with all this?' She gestured around the room, as if rousing them both, reminding them of where they were and how many people were watching.

Both separated a little, straightening in their seats. 'Acknowledging the necessity of something has no bearing on its likely success.'

'I take it back. I think I was right the first time we met. You're a cynic.'

'*That* I have been called frequently.'

The air between them seemed to spark.

Awareness flooded Johara's body. Sitting close to him, speaking like this, she found the tension almost unbearable. She felt as though her skin was alive with an itch that she wanted to scratch and scratch and scratch.

The evening was long. After the dinner—which spanned six courses—there were speeches. The trade minister, the foreign minister, the culture minister. Johara sat beside Amir and listened, a polite smile on her face even when many small, barbed insults were laid at her country's feet. She wanted to respond to each that it took two to tango—a war couldn't be continued at only one country's insistence. Wrongs had been perpetrated on both sides. But all the while, the knowledge of what the man beside her had lost at her uncle's hand kept her silent.

She nodded politely, reminding herself again and again that her place in all this was not to inflame tensions so much as to soothe them. A necessary part of the peace process would involve humility—from both sides. The thought made her smile. Imagining Sheikh Amir Haddad humbling himself was not the easiest thing to do.

Finally, when all the speeches had been made, Johara stood. She ignored the small insults she'd heard and focussed on the bigger picture, and the fact Amir had invited her here.

'I'm gratified to sit here with you as a representative of my brother, Sheikh Malik Qadir, and the people of Taquul. I hope this is the first of many such events enjoyed by our people in this new age of peace and understanding.' She paused and smiled, her eyes skimming the room before coming to rest on Amir. He didn't return her smile and the expression on his chiselled face made her pulse rush through her body. 'I'm grateful for the hospitality of your kingdom, your people, and your Sheikh.' She wrenched her eyes away from him with difficulty. 'I look forward to getting to know the ways of your people better.'

When she sat down, it was to the sound of muted applause. Even that earned a wry smile from her, though she dipped her head forward to hide it. Only Amir caught the look, his eyes still trained on her face.

As was the custom, he led her from the room, the official engagement at an end. It would be ordinary for him to hand her off as soon as they'd left the palace hall, and yet he didn't. He continued to walk with her. On either side, they were flanked by enormous flower arrangements—filled with natives of the region, blooms, foliage, pomegranate, citrus, all in their infancy so the fruit was miniature and fragrant. There were security personnel too, carefully watchful, discreet and respectful, but Amir felt their presence with a growing sense of frustration.

At the bottom of the stairs that led to the wing of the palace reserved for visiting dignitaries, he paused, wondering at the sense of hesitation that gripped him.

'You must be tired.' His voice was gruff. He made an effort to soften it.

'Must I be?' She lifted both brows, her lips pursed.

'You arrived early this morning. It's been a big day.'

'Yes,' she agreed, looking sideways with a small sigh. 'But I'm not tired.'

Neither said anything. He could only look at her, the face held in profile, so beautiful, so achingly beautiful, but so full of the Qadir features that even as he yearned to reach for her he stayed where he was, his body taut, old hatreds deep inside his soul refusing to be quelled.

'In truth, I'm restless,' she said after a moment. 'I feel as though I've spent all day saying and doing what's expected of me and what I'd really like is just a few minutes of being my actual self.'

The confession surprised him.

'I don't suppose you have a maze I could go and get lost in for a bit?'

It was said light-heartedly, as a joke, but he couldn't fail to feel jolted by the reminder of that damned maze.

'No.' Too gruff again. He shook his head. This was no good. How could she be so effortlessly charming despite their long, bitter past? 'We have something even better.'

She put a hand on her hip, drawing his attention downwards, to her waist and the curves that had driven him crazy long before he'd known who she was. 'I doubt that.'

His laugh was deep and throaty. 'Want to bet?'

'Sure. Show me.'

What was he doing? He should tell her to go to bed; in the morning, she'd have another busy day. But a thousand fireworks seemed to be bursting beneath his skin. He wanted to be alone with her, even when he knew every reason he should fight that desire.

'May I go and change first?'

His lips tugged downwards. 'Your Highness, you're here as my guest. You do not need to ask my permission for anything.'

He'd surprised her. She bit down on her lip and he had to look away, before impulses overtook him and he dropped his head to kiss her. It would have felt so natural and easy.

'I'll wait here.'

She nodded once then turned, walking up the wide, sweeping staircase. He couldn't help but watch her departure.

Fifteen minutes later, Johara was ready. Having played the part of dutiful princess all day, she had found it a sheer, blissful relief to slip out of the couture dress she'd worn to the state dinner and pull on a pair of simple black trousers and an emerald-green blouse, teamed with simple black leather ballet flats. It was the kind of outfit she would wear in New York—dressy enough to escape criticism but comfortable and relatable. Her hair had been styled into an elegant braid that wrapped around her head like a crown to secure the actual crown she'd worn—enormous diamonds forming a crescent above her head. She deftly removed the two dozen pins that had been used to secure it, laying the tiara on the dressing table, then letting her hair fall around her shoulders in loose voluminous waves.

With more time, she might have washed her face clean of the make-up she wore, but impatience was guiding her, making her work fast. As she walked back down the staircase, she only had eyes for Amir. He was standing exactly where she'd left him, dressed in the formal robes he'd worn to dinner, his swarthy complexion and the jet black of his hair forming a striking contrast to the snowy white robes.

All night he'd been businesslike, treating her as though they had no history beyond that of their countries, but now, there was more. He was incapable of shielding his response to her—the way his eyes travelled her body with a slow, possessive heat, starting with her face, which he studied with an intensity that took her breath away, then shifting lower, moving over the curves of her breasts, the indent of her waist, the generous swell of her hips, all the way down to her feet as she walked, one step at a time, holding the handrail for fear she might stumble. And as his eyes moved, heat travelled the same path, setting fire to her bloodstream so by the time she reached him she felt as though she were smouldering.

'Well?' Her voice shook a little; she didn't care. 'What do you have to rival the maze?'

His eyes lifted to her lips and she didn't breathe—she couldn't—for several long seconds. Her lungs burned.

He was going to kiss her. His eyes were so intent on her lips, his body so close—when had that even happened?—his expression so loaded with sensuality that memories weaved through her, reminding her of what they'd shared.

She waited, her face upturned, her lips

parted, her blood firing so hard and fast that she could barely think, let alone hear. She knew she should step backwards, move away from him—this was all too complicated—but she couldn't. She wouldn't. Just as the hand of fate seemed to guide them in the maze, a far greater force was at work now.

She expelled a shuddering breath simply because her lungs needed to work, and with the exhalation her body swayed forward a little, not intentionally and not by much, but it brought her to him, her breasts brushing to his chest lightly, so that her nipples hummed at the all too brief contact.

'Johara.' He said her name with intent, with surrender, and with pain. It was all too hard. Where she could push the difficulties aside, at least temporarily, he appeared unable to. He swallowed so his Adam's apple moved visibly, then stepped backwards, his face a mask of discipline, his smile a gash in his handsome face.

Disappointment made her want to howl *No!* into the corridor. She did nothing.

'Your Highness.' He addressed her formally, gesturing with the upturned palm of his hand that she should precede him down the corridor. Her legs felt wobbly and moist heat pooled between her thighs, leaving her in little doubt of just how desperately she wanted him.

She moved in the direction he'd indicated, and when he fell into step beside her he walked closely, close enough that their arms brushed with each stride, so heat and tension began to arrow through her, spreading butterflies of desire and hope in her gut. But why hope? What did she want? He was—or had been until recently—the enemy.

Not my enemy.

No, not her enemy. Though she'd accepted the war between their countries and the family feud that had defined the Qadirs and Haddads for generations, she had felt no personal hatred for him, nor his parents. The fact their countries had been at war until recently wasn't enough of a reason to ignore her instincts and her desires.

But for Amir, their history was so much worse. Where she had no personal wrong to resent him for, he'd lost his parents because of her uncle's malicious cruelty. His hatred for her family was understandable. But did he have to include her in that?

What did she want? The question kept circling around and around and around her mind, with no answer in sight. After several minutes, they reached a wide-set doorway, thrown open to the desert evening. He stood, waiting for her to move through it first, his manners innate and old-fashioned.

She stepped into the cool night air as Amir spoke to the servants. 'We are not to be followed.'

There was a pause and then a deferential nod of agreement. Johara turned away, amused to imagine what they must think—their Sheikh going out of the palace with a Qadir? Did they suspect Johara, all five and a half feet of her, posed a threat to the man?

Her lips curved in a smile at the notion, a smile that still hovered on her lips when he joined her. 'Care to share the joke?'

'I was just thinking how suspicious your guards looked,' she murmured, nudging him with her elbow, so his eyes fell to hers. Heat passed between them.

'You are from Taquul,' he said simply.

She ignored the implication. 'As though I might have a three-foot scabbard buried in here somewhere.' She ran her hands over her hips, shaking her head at the preposterous idea.

'I take it you don't?'

Her laugh was soft. 'You're welcome to check, Amir.'

As soon as she said the words she wished she could unsay them. She lifted a hand to her lips and stopped walking, staring at him with eyes that offered a silent apology. 'I didn't mean for you to…'

But he stared at her with a look that was impossible to read, his breath audible in the stillness of the night.

'It wasn't an invitation?'

Her heart was beating way too fast. How could it continue at that pace?

'We agreed that night was a mistake,' she reminded him.

'No, *I* said it was a mistake. *You* said it felt right.'

Her lips parted at the reminder. 'Yes, I did say that.'

He turned to look back to the palace. They'd moved down the steps and into a garden fragrant with night-flowering jasmine and citrus blossoms, out of sight of the guards. But he turned, moving them further, into an area overgrown with trees. It was unlike the maze in Taquul. Where that was all manicured and enchanting for its formal shape—like a perfect outdoor room—this was more akin to something from a fairy tale. Ancient trees with trunks as wide as six of Amir's chests grew gnarled and knotted towards a sky she knew to be there only because it *must* be there, not because she could see it. The foliage of each tree formed a thick canopy, creating an atmosphere of darkness. Were it not for Amir's hand, which he extended to take hers, she might have lost her footing and fallen. But he guided her expertly, leading her along a narrow path as if by memory. Deeper in the forest, the beautiful fragrance grew thicker and here there was a mesmerising birdcall, like a bell and a whip, falling at once. She paused to listen to it.

'The *juniya*.' He said the word as most people said her name, with a soft inflection on the 'j', so it was more like 'sh'.

'*Juniya,*' she repeated, listening as at least two of them began to sing back and forth.

'They're native to this forest. In our most ancient texts they are spoken of, depicted in some of the first scrolls of the land. But they exist only here, in the trees that surround the palace.'

'I can't believe how verdant the land is here.' She shook her head. 'It's like the foot of the mountains.'

'That's where the water comes from.'

'The moat around the palace?'

'And in my private hall,' he agreed, reminding her of the little stream that flowed through that magical place he'd taken her to when first she'd arrived at the palace—had that only been earlier on this same day? 'There's an underground cavern that reaches the whole way; the river travels through it. In ancient times, it was used to send spies into Taquul,' he said with a tight smile she could just make out. They con-

tinued to walk once more, and eventually the
canopy grew less apparent, light from the stars
and moon reaching them, so she could see his
face more clearly.

'But not any more?'

'It's more closely guarded on the other side.'
He laughed. 'And our own guards do the same,'
he added, perhaps wondering if she might take
the information back to her brother, to use it
as a tactical strength against him. The thought
brought a soft sigh to her lips.

'Even now in peace?' she prompted him.

'Always.' The words vibrated with the depth
of his seriousness. 'The water runs underground
to the palace, the heart of our government. We
will protect it with our lives.'

A shiver ran down her spine, his passion ig-
niting something inside her.

'The war went on for a long time. It's only
natural to think like that.'

'You consider yourself immune from the ef-
fects of it?'

She lifted her slender shoulders. 'I've spent
a lot of time in New York. In truth, I've always
felt I straddled two worlds, with one foot in
my Taquul heritage and another in my mother's America. That isn't to say I feel the connection to my people any less, nor that I don't
see the seriousness of the war, but I see it—at

times—with something akin to an outsider's perspective.'

He reached out and grabbed an overhanging leaf, running his fingertips over it before handing it to Johara. She took it, lifting it her nose and inhaling gratefully. The smell was sweet and intoxicating. 'With an outsider's clarity, perhaps,' he said darkly.

It jolted her gaze to his face. 'You think I have greater clarity than you in this matter?'

He stopped walking, his expression tight. 'I think war has become a way of life,' he said with a nod. 'Like you said. Those habits will die hard.'

'It's ironic,' she murmured softly, 'that you remind me of him, in many ways.'

He braced. 'Who?'

'My brother.'

His expression was forbidding. 'I'm not sure I appreciate that.'

'I didn't expect you would, but it's true. I think it's probably an important thing to remember in war. You were the one who said that— we're more alike than we are different.'

'I was speaking generally.'

She shrugged once more. 'And I'm speaking specifically.'

'Don't.' He shook his head, his eyes locked to hers. 'Don't compare me to him.'

'He's my brother,' she reminded him. 'You can stand here with me, showing me this incredible place—' she gestured beyond her '—but you can't even speak his name?'

Amir stiffened. 'Believe me, Johara, I am conscious, every minute we're together, of who you are and what my being here with you means. You think I don't feel that I am, right this second, betraying my parents' memory?'

She sucked in a jagged breath, pain lancing her at the fact he could perceive anything to do with her as a betrayal of his parents. She spun away from him, looking back towards the palace. It was too far to see. She knew it would be there, beyond the enormous trees, glowing like a golden beacon. But it was no beacon, really. Not for her. The pain would be impossible to escape so long as she was here in Ishkana.

Her voice wobbled. 'I think you're honouring their memory by striving for peace. I think they'd be proud of you.'

His breath was ragged, filling the air behind her. His hand curved around her wrist, spinning her gently back to face him. 'Perhaps,' he agreed. 'But that doesn't make this any easier.'

His face showed the burden of his thoughts, the weight of his grief. She looked at him for several seconds and then went to pull her wrist away. He didn't release her.

'You are a Qadir,' he said darkly, as if reminding himself.

She lifted her chin, fixing him with a determined glance. 'And you are a Haddad. What's your point?'

'When my parents died, I could not show how I felt. I was twelve years old—still a child—but, here in Ishkana, old enough to become Sheikh. My life changed in a thousand ways. There was no time to grieve, to mourn, to process the loss of my parents. We were at war.' His thumb began to pad the flesh of her inner wrist, rhythmically, softly, but almost as though he didn't realise he was doing it.

'I used to fall asleep at night with only one thought to comfort me.'

A lump had formed in her throat, making it difficult to swallow. 'What was that?'

'That I would hate the Qadirs and what they had done for the rest of my life.' His eyes seemed to probe hers, his expression tense—his whole body, in fact, radiated with tension.

'You were twelve.' The words came out as a whisper. She cleared her throat and tried again. 'Of course you were angry.'

'Not angry,' he corrected. 'I was calm. Resolute. Determined.' When he breathed, his chest moved, brushing her.

'And yet you've signed a peace treaty.'

'For as much as I hate your family, I love my country and its people. For them I will always do what is best.'

Her heart felt as though it were bursting into a thousand pieces. Her stomach hurt. 'I don't know what to say.' She dropped her gaze to his chest, unable to bear his scrutiny for a moment longer. 'My uncle was imprisoned by my family after his despicable action—where he still languishes, at my brother's behest. He had no support from my parents, my brother, and certainly not from me. Our war was an economic one, a war of sanctions rather than violence.' She tilted her head, willing his defiance. 'Oh, there are the renegades on the borders and of course the military posturing that seems to go hand in hand with war, but to stoop to something so violent and…and…wrong as assassinating your parents? That was my uncle's madness, Amir. If you are to hate anyone—and I cannot stress enough how futile and damaging that kind of hatred is—but if you insist on hating anyone, have it be Johar. Not every single person who shares his surname. Not me.'

He groaned, low and deep in his throat. 'What you say makes perfect sense.'

'And yet you don't agree?' Her words sounded bleak.

'I don't *want* to agree.'

She lifted her eyes back to his. 'Why not?'

'Because this ancient hatred I feel is the only thing that's been stopping me from doing what I wanted to do the second you arrived at the palace this morning.'

Her heart stopped racing. It thudded to a slow stop. 'Which is?'

His eyes dropped to her lips. 'I want to kiss you, Johara.'

Her heart stammered.

'I want to claim your mouth with mine. I want to lace my fingers through your hair and hold your head still so I can taste every piece of you, bit by bit, until you are moaning and begging me, surrendering to me completely as you did in the maze.'

Her knees were knocking together wildly, her stomach filled with a kaleidoscope of butterflies.

'I want to strip these clothes from your body and make love to you right here, with only this ancient forest to bear witness to whatever madness this is.'

She could barely breathe, let alone form words. 'Would that be so bad?'

His eyes closed, as if it were the worst thing she could have said. 'The first time was a mistake, but I didn't know who you were then.'

'Now you do, and you still want me,' she

challenged softly, aware she was walking on the edge of a precipice, so close to tumbling over.

He swore softly in one of the dialects of his people. 'You deserve better than this. Better than for a man who can offer you nothing, wanting you for your body.'

She didn't—couldn't—respond to that.

'I can offer you nothing,' he reiterated. 'No future, no friendship beyond what is expected of us in our position. I cannot—will not—form any relationship that might jeopardise what I owe my people.'

'Damn it, Amir, I have no intention of doing anything to hurt your people...'

'Caring for you would compromise my ability to rule. There are lines here we cannot cross.'

She swallowed, the words he spoke so difficult to comprehend and yet, at the same time, on an instinctive level, they made an awful kind of sense. Amir had been running this country since he was twelve years old. His life was impossible for Johara to understand. But she knew about duty and sacrifice; she had seen both these traits ingrained into her brother, she understood how his country would always come first.

And it wasn't that he perceived *her* as a threat to the country. Not Johara, as a woman. Johara as a Qadir, as a member of the Taquul royal family. It was symbolic. The peace was new.

His people would take time to accept it, to trust it, and if news of an affair between Amir and Johara were to break, it could threaten everything by stirring up strong negative feelings in response. Retaliation could occur.

The war had been too costly, especially on the border.

She closed her eyes and nodded, a sad shift of her head, because the futility of it all felt onerous and cumbersome.

'I don't hate you, Amir.' She pulled her hand out of his and this time he let her. Her flesh screamed in agony, begging to be back in his grip. Her stomach looped again and again. 'But you're right. I deserve better than to be the scapegoat for all the pain you've suffered in your life.' She straightened her spine and looked beyond him. 'Shall we go back to the palace now? I think I've seen enough for tonight.'

CHAPTER SIX

THE SUN WAS UNRELENTING, the sands from the
deserts stirred into a frenzy and reaching them
even here, on the outskirts of the city where one
of the oldest libraries stood in existence. He'd
had this added to the itinerary days before she
arrived. Memories of the maze had been running thick and fast through his mind. The pride
with which she'd spoken of her work with childhood literacy had been impossible to forget—
her eyes had sparkled like diamonds when she'd
discussed the initiative she'd put together.

He knew she'd find the library itself beautiful—the building was very old, the books,
parchments, scrolls, tapestries and stone walls
contained within dated back thousands of years,
but more than that, there were the spaces that
had been built in the last fifteen years, during
his reign, specifically to make books and reading more accessible to the youth of Ishkana.

This was the last stop on what had been a

day filled with formal events. So much polite meeting and greeting, smiling, posing for photographs, and all the while Johara's features had never shown a hint of strain or discomfort. Not at the proximity to a man who had been, as she claimed, using her as a 'scapegoat'. Nor in exhaustion from the heat, nor after hours on her feet in dainty high heels that must surely pinch.

Even now, she listened with a rapt expression on her face as his Minister for the Arts explained how the library spaces worked.

Impatience coursed through Amir's veins. He no longer wanted to stand to the side as she was shown through the library. He wished everyone to leave, so that it was just Johara and him, so that Amir could tell her what he'd hoped when he'd had the rooms built, so that he could tell her his favourite memories of being here in this building. Even when he was a boy, it had been one of his most delighted-in haunts.

'What an incredible programme,' she said, almost wistfully, running a finger over the bottom of a windowsill. Beyond them, the classroom was full of children—some of the poorest of Ishkana. Buses were sent each morning to various districts, a bell loudly proclaiming its arrival, giving all children who wished it a chance to get on board.

'We are working towards universal education,' Amir found himself saying, moving closer, half closing the Minister for the Arts from the conversation and drawing Johara's eyes to his. It was only then that a sense of reserve entered her expression—just a hint of caution in the depths of her eyes but enough for him to see it and recognise it. 'It was a passion of my father's.' He took a step down the marble corridor, urging her to follow him. It was impossible not to remember the group that followed them—staff, servants, media—and yet he found himself tuning them out, thinking only of Johara as they walked.

'Education?' she prompted, falling into step beside him.

'Yes. The benefits to the whole country can't be underestimated.'

'I agree,' she said, almost wistfully.

'This is the state library,' he continued. 'So we were limited in the scope of what we could achieve. Naturally there is much here that is protected from too much public access—the oldest texts are stored on the second and third floors and kept out of the way of children.' His smile was genuine.

She nodded. 'Naturally.'

'This is just an example of what we're prioritising, and serves only the inner-city children. Beyond this, we've built twenty-seven libraries in the last decade, starting in the poorest regional communities and working our way up. The libraries aren't just for books, though. There are computers and tablets, lessons in how to use both, and for the children, six days per week, classes are offered. Book hiring is incentivised, with small tax breaks offered to regular borrowers.'

She gasped. 'Really?'

'Oh, yes. Really.'

'What an incredible initiative.'

He lifted his shoulders. 'Reading is a habit that brings with it many benefits.'

She seemed to miss her step a little. He reached out and put a hand under her elbow, purely to steady her, but the sparks that shot through him warned him from making such a stupid mistake—particularly in public.

'You must feel likewise to have established your childhood literacy initiative?'

'Yes.' Her smile was more natural. She casually pulled her arm away, putting a little more distance between them.

'You enjoy reading?'

She kept her eyes straight ahead, and didn't answer. Instead, after a moment, they came to the opening of a large room, this one filled with straight desks at which students could study during term time, and dark wooden walls filled with reference texts.

'What a lovely room.'

He wondered if she was changing the subject intentionally, but let it go. There would be time later to ask her again—he wasn't sure why it mattered, only it felt as if she was hiding something from him and he didn't want that. He wanted to know…everything.

The thought almost made *him* miss a step, for how unwelcome it was.

Why? What was the point? He didn't want to analyse it, he knew only that his instincts were pushing him towards her, not away, and he could no longer tell what was right or wrong.

The rest of the library tour took forty-five minutes. At the end of it, he paused, with one look keeping the rest of their contingent at a distance, leading her away separately. 'Would you like to see what's upstairs?'

'The ancient texts?'

He dipped his head.

'I…would have thought they were too precious to share with someone like me.'

His stomach tightened. Because she was a Qadir? Why wouldn't she feel like that, particularly after the things he'd said the night before? 'They are not something we routinely display to foreign guests.' He deliberately appeared to mis-understand her. 'But would you like to see them?'

Her breath grew louder, her eyes uncertain. He could feel a battle raging within her, the same kind of battle that was being fought inside him. 'I would,' she said, finally, not meeting his eyes.

Without a response to her, he spun on his heel and stalked to the group. He addressed only Ahmed, giving brief instructions that the mo-torcade should wait twenty minutes—that he and the Princess were not to be disturbed.

It was a break from protocol, but nothing he couldn't explain later.

Before he could see the look of disapproval on Ahmed's face, Amir walked Johara towards a bank of elevators, pressing a button that im-mediately summoned a carriage. The doors swished open and he waited for her to step in-side before joining her and pressing a gold but-ton. Even the elevators were very old, built at the turn of the nineteenth and twentieth centu-ries. It chugged slowly, and he tried not to pay attention to how close they stood in the confines of the infrastructure.

The doors opened and he felt relief—relief to be able to step further away from her, to stop breathing in her scent, to be able to resist the impulse to touch her, just because she happened to be standing right in front of him.

'Many of these are relevant to your country,' he said, indicating one tapestry that hung opposite the elevator, dimly lit with overhead lights to preserve its beautiful threads.

She studied the pictures, a look of fascination on her features. He led her through the area, showing some of his favourite pieces.

'You sound as though you know this place like the back of your hand,' she said after ten minutes.

He smiled. 'I do. I came here often as a child. I loved to sit up here and read while my parents attended to business at parliament. I was fortunate that they indulged my every whim.' He laughed.

Her tone was teasing. 'Are you saying you were spoiled?'

'Actually, I wasn't.' He grinned. 'Only in this aspect—my mother found my love of books amusing.'

'Why?'

'Because for the most part, I preferred to be out of doors. I hated restriction. I liked to run and ride and swim and climb. In that way, I was cast in my father's image. But then, here at the library, I saw the opening to all these other worlds and found a different way to run and be free.'

She was transfixed by his words, her expression completely engaged by what he was saying. 'It was a catalyst for them. Seeing how I loved these texts, how they opened my eyes and mind—I still remember the conversation between them, travelling back to the palace one night, when my father remarked that every child should be able to lose themselves in a library as I seemed to want to.'

Johara paused, looking at a small book with a golden spine and beautiful cursive script.

'They were right.' Her voice was small.

'Was this similar to your own childhood?'

A beat passed, a pause which seemed somehow unnatural. 'I…spent my childhood undertaking ceremonial duties on behalf of the palace,' she said calmly. But too calm, as though her voice was carefully neutralised to hide any real feeling. He didn't speak, sensing that she would continue only if he stayed silent.

He was right. 'My mother died when I was six. I have vague memories of attending events with her. But after she passed, I was expected to take on her role.' Her smile was laced with mockery. 'Something you know about.'

'At such a young age?'

'I didn't question it at the time. My *amalä* had focussed a lot of my education on etiquette, socialising, on how to speak and be spoken to.'

She shrugged as though it didn't matter. 'It was second nature to me.'

'But you were still a baby.'

She laughed. 'I was old enough.' Her brow furrowed. 'There wasn't much time for libraries and reading, nor even for studying. None of which was deemed particularly important for me anyway.'

Amir stopped walking, something like anger firing through him. 'So your education was sacrificed in order for you to cut ribbons and make speeches?'

'I sit on the board of many important charities and foundations,' she contradicted defensively, then dropped her head in a silent sign of concession. 'But yes. Essentially, you're correct.'

'And your brother?' He couldn't conceal his anger then. It whipped them both, drawing them closer without their knowledge.

'Mal had an education similar to yours, I imagine. Well rounded, with the best tutors in various subjects being flown in to instruct him. He was taught to be a statesman, a philosopher, to govern and preside over the country from when he was a very young boy.'

Amir wanted to punch something! 'That's grossly unfair.'

Johara's eyes flashed to his; he felt her agreement and surprise. 'It's the way of my people.'

'It's as though nothing has changed for *your people* in the last one hundred years.'

She lifted her shoulders. 'And Ishkana is so different?'

He stared at her as though she had lost her mind. 'Yes, Ishkana is different. You've seen the facilities we've created. You've heard me talk about the importance of books and education for children. Have you heard me say, at any point, "for boys", as opposed to "children"?'

She didn't speak. Her eyes held his, and something sparked between them.

'My grandfather made inroads to gender equality, but he was hampered—if you can believe it—by public opinions. By the time my father was Sheikh, the Internet had been born, and a homogenisation of attitudes was—I would have thought—inevitable. My mother was progressive, and fiercely intelligent. The idea of her skill set languishing simply because women weren't seen as having the same rights to education as men...'

'I am not languishing,' she interrupted. 'I get to represent causes that matter a great deal to me.'

He stared at her, not wanting to say what he was thinking, knowing his assessment would hurt her.

'What?' she demanded. 'Say what you're thinking.'

Surprise made him cough. How could she

read him so well? What was this magic that burst around them, making him feel as though they were connected in a way that transcended everything he knew he *should* feel about her?

'Only that it sounds to me as though your representation is more about your position and recognisability than anything else.'

She jerked her head back as though he'd slapped her and he instantly wish he hadn't said such a cruel thing. He shook his head, moving a step closer, his lips pressed together.

'I'm sorry.'

'Don't.' She lifted a hand to his chest, her own breathing ragged. 'Don't apologise.'

They stood like that, so close, bodies melded, breath mingling, eyes latched, until Johara made a sort of strangled noise and stepped backwards, her spine connected with the firmness of a white marble wall.

'Don't apologise,' she said again, this time quieter, more pained. He echoed her movement, stepping towards her, his body trapping hers where it was, his own responding with a jerk of awareness he wished he could quell.

'You're right.' She bit down on her full lower lip, reminding her of the way she'd done that in the maze, and the way he'd sought it with his own teeth. 'I'm ornamental. Unlike your mother, I'm not fiercely intelligent. I can't even read properly, Amir. Educating me in a traditional way would have been a waste of effort. So my parents focussed on what I was good at, at my strengths—which is people. I serve my country in this way.'

He could hardly breathe, let alone speak. 'You were not even taught to read?'

'I was taught,' she corrected. 'But not well, and it didn't seem to matter until I was much older. At twelve, I sat some tests—and was diagnosed with severe dyslexia.' A crease formed between her brows. 'It wouldn't have made any difference if they'd discovered it earlier. It's not curable. My brain is wired differently from yours. I can read—passably—but it takes me longer than you can imagine and it will never be what I do for pleasure.' Her eyes tangled with his and she shook her head. 'Don't look at me like that.'

'How am I looking at you?' he interrogated gently.

'As though you pity me.' She pressed her teeth into her lip once more. 'I still love books— I listen to recordings whenever I can—and let me assure you, I derive the same pleasure from their pages as you do.'

He listened, but something was flaring inside him, something he hadn't felt in such a raw and violent form for a very long time. Admiration. Respect.

'This is why you founded the literacy initiative in New York?'

'Yes.' Her smile, as he focussed conversation on something that brought her joy, almost stole his breath. 'To help children. Even children like I was—if a diagnosis can be made early enough—will be spared years of feeling that they're not good enough, or smart enough.'

'And you felt these things.'

Her smile dropped. His anger was back—anger at her parents, and, because they were dead and no longer able to account for their terrible, neglectful parenting, anger at the brother who hadn't troubled himself to notice Johara's struggles.

'Yes.' Her eyes held defiance. 'I *used* to feel that way. But then I moved to America and I came to understand that the skills I have cannot be taught. I'm great with people. I'm great at fundraising. I can work a room and secure millions of dollars in donations in the space of a couple of hours. I can make a real difference in the world, Amir, so please, for the love of everything you hold dear, stop looking at me as though I'm an object of pity or—'

Something in the region of his chest tightened. 'Or?'

'Or I'll… I don't know. Stamp my foot. Or

scream.' She shook her head. 'Just don't you dare pity me.'

He gently took her chin between his finger and thumb. 'I don't pity you, Johara.' His eyes roamed her face and, in the distance, he could hear the beating of a drum, low and solid, the tempo rhythmic and urgent all at once. It took him moments to realise there was no drum, just the beating of his heart, the torrent of his pulse slamming through his body.

'You don't?'

'I admire you,' he admitted gruffly. 'I admire the hell out of you and damn it if I don't want to kiss you more than ever right now.'

Her knees could barely hold her. If he weren't standing so close, pinning her to the wall, she wasn't sure she would have trusted her legs to keep her upright. His face was so close, his lips just an inch from hers. She tilted her face, her own lips parting in an unspoken invitation, and she stared at him, hoping, wanting, every fibre of her being reverberating with need.

'How do you make me forget so easily?'

'Forget what?' Closer. Did she lift onto the tips of her toes or did he lower his face? Either way, her mouth could almost brush his now. Adrenalin surged through her veins, fierce and loud.

'Who you are.' He threw the words aside as

though they were inconsequential, and then finally he kissed her, a kiss that was for him exultant and for her drugging. Her need for him obliterated every shred of rational thought, every ability to process what was happening. But even as his tongue slid between her lips, tangling with hers, and his knee nudged her legs apart, propping her up, her sluggish brain threaded his simple statement together. *Who you are.*

Who she was. It was so fundamental—her parentage, her lineage, her place in the Taquul royal family.

His hands gripped her hips, holding her possessively and almost fearfully, as though she might move away from him; he held her as though his life depended on her nearness. His kiss stole her breath and gave her life. She lifted her hands, tangling them behind his neck, her fingers running into the nape of his hair, pressing her breasts against his chest, her nipples tingling with remembered sensations.

How do you make me forget so easily?

But they couldn't forget. It wasn't that easy. He was a Haddad and she a Qadir and somewhere over the last one hundred years it had been written in stone that they should hate each other. Yet she didn't. She couldn't hate him. He'd done her no wrong and, more than that, she'd seen qualities that made her feel the opposite of hate. She *liked* him. She enjoyed spending time with him. She found talking to him hypnotic and addictive. And kissing him like this lit a thousand fires in the fabric of her soul.

But Amir would never accept her. He would always resent her, and possibly hate her. And that hatred would destroy her if she wasn't very, very careful. And what of her brother if he learned of this? Even her defiant streak didn't run that deep.

With every single scrap of willpower she possessed, Johara drew her hands between them and pushed at his chest, just enough to separate them, to give her breathing space.

'Your Majesty.' She intentionally used his title, needing to remind him of what he claimed she made him forget. 'Nothing has changed since last night.' She waited, her eyes trying to read his face, to understand him better. 'Has it?'

His eyes widened, as though her reminder had caught him completely unawares. She could feel the power of his arousal between her legs, and knew how badly he wanted her. Yet he stepped backwards immediately, rubbing his palm over his chin.

'You're right, Princess.' His smile was self-mocking. 'That won't happen again.'

CHAPTER SEVEN

'IT'S ONLY THREE more days.' Malik's voice came down the phone line, in an attempt to offer comfort. He could have no way of knowing that, far from placating her, the reminder that the week she'd been invited to Ishkana for was halfway over would spark something a little like depression inside her belly.

She looked out of her magnificent bedroom window over an aviary very like the one in Taquul, and again felt how alike these two countries were—just as Amir had said.

'I know.' It was the end of a busy day, filled with commitments and engagements. She'd seen so much of the city, met so many politicians and leaders, and the more she saw of this country, the less contented she felt.

The war had been so futile.

This was a beautiful country, a beautiful people. They'd been hurt by the past, just as the people in Taquul had been. Not for the first time, frustration with her parents and grandparents gnawed at her. Why hadn't they been able to find a peaceful resolution sooner? Why had it rested on two men, one hundred years after the first shot was fired?

'What's it like?'

'It's...' A movement below caught her attention. She swept her gaze downwards, trying to catch it again. Something white in amongst the olive and pomegranate trees below. Another movement. Her heart recognised before her mind did.

Amir.

He moved purposefully towards one of the aviaries, his frame powerful, his movements everything that was masculine and primal. He opened the door, and made a gesture with his hand. A large bird, with a wingspan half the height of Amir, flew from the cage and did a circle above his head, above Johara, its eyes surveying what they could, before neatly returning and hooking its claws around Amir's outstretched arm. Its feathers were a pale, pearlescent cream with small flecks of light brown, its beak tipped in grey.

'What?' Malik was impatient. 'Terrible? Awful? Are you hating it?'

'No!' She had forgotten all about her brother, on the other end of the phone. She shook her head despite the fact he wasn't there to see her. 'It's…wonderful.'

Amir's lips moved; he was speaking to the bird. She wished, more than anything, that she could hear what he was saying.

'Wonderful?' Malik's surprise was obvious. She ignored it.

'Yes. I have to go now.'

'But—'

'I'll call you another time, okay?' She pressed the red button on her screen, her eyes fixed on Amir. She could not look away. The dusk sky created a dramatic backdrop to an already overpoweringly dramatic scene. With the falcon perched on his forearm, he looked every bit the powerful Emir. She held her breath as he began to move towards the palace, her eyes following every athletic step he took, her mind silently willing him to look towards her, to see her. And do what? She stared at him as though with her eyes alone she could summon him.

When he was almost beneath her, he looked up, his eyes sweeping the windows of her suite before locking to her. He stopped walking, and he stared at her as she had been staring at him.

Hungrily.

Urgently.

As though seeing one another were their sole means of survival.

He dipped his head a moment later, a bow of respect, and her heart stammered; he was going to go away again. She wanted to scream. Impatience and frustration were driving her mad. Since their kiss in the library, she'd barely seen him. Brief photo opportunities and nothing more. And at these interludes he was polite but went out of his way to keep a distance, not touching her, his smile barely reaching his eyes before he replaced it with a businesslike look.

But here, now, the same fire that had burned between them in the library arced through the sky, threatening to singe her nerve endings.

'I...' She said it so quietly she wasn't sure he'd hear. And she had no idea what she even wanted to say. Only that she didn't want him to walk away from her.

His eyes lifted, held hers a moment, and then he grimaced, as though he was fighting a war within himself. A moment later, he began to walk, disappearing from her view completely. She stamped her foot on the balcony and squeezed her eyes shut, gripping the railing tightly. Her heart was frantic and, ridiculously, stupid tears filled her throat with salt, threatening to douse her eyes. She blinked rapidly to ward them off, hating how he could affect her, hating how futile their situation was. Of all the men she had to meet, of all the men who had the ability to make her crazy with desire, why did it have to be a king who saw himself as her sworn enemy? A man who had every reason in the world to hate her family?

With a growling sound of impatience she stalked back into the beautiful suite of rooms she'd been appointed, deciding she'd take a cool shower. Three more days. She could get through this. And then what? Forget about Amir?

Her skin lifted with goosebumps. Unbidden, memories of the maze flooded her mind, filling her eyes with visions of him over her, his handsome, symmetrical face, she felt the movements of his body in hers, and she groaned, the shower forgotten. She closed her eyes, allowing the memories to overtake her, reliving that experience breath by breath until her skin was flushed and her blood boiling in her veins.

She would never forget about him. She would return to Taquul and he would return with her—a part of him would anyway. What they'd shared had been so brief yet in some vital way he'd become a part of her soul.

A knock drew her from her reverie. She turned her attention to the door, wondering what she must look like—a quick glance in the mirror confirmed her cheeks were flushed and her eyes sparkling. She pressed the backs of her hands to her cheeks, sucked in a breath and then opened the door.

If she'd been hoping for Amir—and of course, on some level, she had been—she was to be disappointed. A guard stood there, his impressive military medals on one shoulder catching her eye. Medals that had been won in the service of his army—against her country. Another blip of frustration. The war was over now, but the hurts went deep on both sides. Did this soldier hate her because of who she was and where she came from? It was impossible to tell. His face was impassive as he held a piece of cream paper towards her, folded into quarters.

'Thank you,' she murmured, offering him a smile—perhaps enough smiles given genuinely and freely could turn hatred to acceptance, and eventually fondness.

She waited until the door was clicked shut again, then unfolded the note.

Come to the West Gate. A

Owing to her dyslexia and his hastily scrawled handwriting, it took her several moments to read it and when she finished, her fingertips were unsteady, her breathing even more so. She flicked another glance to the mirror, running her hands across the simple outfit she wore—loose pants and a tunic—then over her hair, which was loose around her shoulders. She reached for some pins and secured it in a low bun, added a hint of lipstick and then moved to the door.

Athena was coming in as Johara opened the door.

'Your Highness? You're going somewhere?'

'I— For a walk,' she said with a small nod.

'Shall I accompany you?'

'No.' Johara's smile was reassuring, when inside she was panicking. The company of her servant—even one she considered a friend, like Athena—was the last thing Johara wanted! 'I'd like to be alone,' she softened the rebuke, reaching out and touching Athena's forearm. 'Goodnight.'

The West Gate was not difficult to find. She had a vague recollection of it having been pointed out to her on her first day, when she'd been given a thorough tour of the palace. She retraced the steps she remembered, until she reached a wall of white marble that stretched almost impenetrably towards the sky, creating a strong barrier to the outside world. Halfway along the wall there was a gate made of gold and bronze, solid and beautiful, with ancient calligraphy inscribed in its centre.

As she approached it she slowed, scanning for Amir. She couldn't see him. But to the right of the enormous gates there was a doorway, made to blend in completely with the wall. It was ajar. She moved towards it, then pushed at it. Amir stood waiting for her.

Her breath hitched in her throat. She'd come so quickly she hadn't paused to consider what she might say to him when she arrived.

Neither smiled.

'Thank you for coming.'

A frown quirked her brows. Had he thought she might not?

'You mentioned that you wanted to see the ruins of *wasat*. They're at their best at sunset.'

It was then that she became aware of a magnificent stallion behind him. Beneath the saddle there was a blanket over its back, gold and black, and a roll of fabric hung to one side. She could only imagine it contained the sorts of necessities one might need when riding horses in this harsh climate—water, a satellite phone.

'Are they—far from here?'

'No.' He gestured to the horse. 'Ride with me.'

It was a command. A shiver ran down her spine, and a whisper of anticipation. She eyed the horse, trying to remember the last time she'd been on the back of one—years. Many, many years. Her gaze flicked uncertainly to his.

'It's like riding a bike,' he said, a smile lifting his lips now, a smile that sent little bubbles popping inside her belly.

She walked towards the horse. It was magnificent. A shimmering black, it reminded her of a George Stubbs painting—all rippling muscles and intelligent eyes. She lifted a hand and ran it over his nose. The horse made a breathy noise of approval then dipped his head.

Amir watched, transfixed.

'He's beautiful.'

'He likes you,' Amir murmured, moving closer, pressing his own hand to the horse's mane, running his fingers over the coarse hair. 'Let me help you up.'

She was tempted to demur, but, looking at the sheer size of the horse, she knew it wouldn't be wise. Or possible.

'Thank you.'

He came to her side, his eyes probing hers. 'Ready?'

She nodded wordlessly.

He caught her around the waist easily, lifting her towards the horse so she could push one leg over and straddle it. Amir's hands lingered on her hips a moment longer than was necessary and still she resented the necessity of their removal.

A moment later, he'd pressed his foot into a stirrup and swung his leg over, nestling in behind her, reaching around and taking the reins, his body framing hers completely. She closed her eyes, praying for strength, because sitting this close to him was its own form of torment. She could smell him, feel him, his touch confident and reassuring as he moved his leg to start the horse in motion.

'We'll go fast,' he said into her ear, the words warm against her flesh. Her heart turned over. She nodded, incapable of speaking.

They sped. The horse galloped north, towards the Al'amanï ranges before tacking east. The sun was low in the sky, the colours spectacular as day blurred towards night. They rode for twenty minutes, each step of the horse jolting Johara against Amir, so after a while she surrendered to the sheer physicality of this, and allowed herself to enjoy it. The feeling of his chest against her back. His thighs against hers. His arms around her, flexing the reins. Every jolt bumped her against him and by the time he brought the horse to a stop, she was so overcome by the sensations that were flooding her body she barely realised they were at an ancient site.

'These are the ruins,' he said, his face forward, beside hers, so if she turned her head just a little her lips would press against his. She could hardly breathe. Her eyes traced the out-lines of the ancient building, barely registering the details. She saw the pillars and columns, one of the ornate rooftops remained, the windows carved into arches. Yes, she could imagine this would have been a resting point in the desert, thousands of years earlier. A lodging as a mid-way point across the landscape. It was beautiful but she was so overwhelmed, it was impossible to react. A noise overhead caught her attention. She glanced up to see the enormous wingspan of a bird—his falcon. As she watched, it came down to land atop the ruins, its eyes surveying the desert.

'They're...' She searched for the word and in-stinctively looked towards Amir. It was a mis-take. Just as she'd imagined, he was so close, and in turning her head towards him she almost brushed his cheek with her lips. He shifted a lit-tle, so that he was facing her, their eyes only an inch apart. The air around them crackled with a heat that had nothing to do with the desert.

'The ruins are...'

She still couldn't find the words. Every cell of her DNA was absorbed by this man. He was too close. Too much. He was...perfect. Super-latives were something she had in abundance, when it came to Amir. The ruins just couldn't compete with him.

'Would you like to see inside?'

No. She wanted to stay right where she was. She bit down on her lip, sure what she was feeling must be obvious in her expression.

'I—' She frowned, her brows drawing together.

'The view from the top is worth seeing.'

Was he oblivious to the tension that was wrapping around her? Did he not feel it?

She nodded slowly, awkwardly, but when he climbed down from the horse she had to tilt her face away from him because of the disappointment she was sure must show in her features. He held his hands out. 'May I?'

He was asking to touch her, again. The small sign of respect came naturally to him.

'Please.' She nodded.

He reached out and took hold of her curved hips, guiding her off the horse. The act brought her body to his, sliding down his length, so a heat that was impossible to ignore began to burn between her legs. She stood there, staring up at him, the sky bathing them in shades of violet and orange, the first stars beginning to twinkle overhead.

'Why did you bring me here?'

A muscle jerked low in his jaw. She dropped her eyes to it, fascinated. Her fingertips itched to reach up and touch, to explore the planes of his face, to feel him with her eyes closed and see him as he'd been in the maze.

'You wanted to see it.'

Her lips twisted in a half-smile. 'There are many things I want to see.'

'This was easy to arrange.'

The answer disappointed her. He was right. This had been easy—a short ride across the desert. He'd undoubtedly wanted to give the bird an outing—bringing Johara was just an afterthought.

It meant nothing to him. She was embarrassing herself by making it into more.

His voice rumbled through her doubts. 'And I wanted to see it with you. Through your eyes.' And then, with a frown, he lifted his hand to lightly caress her cheek. 'I wanted to see your wonderment as you looked upon the ruins. I wanted to be here with you.'

Disappointment evaporated; pleasure soared in its place.

He dropped his hand and took a step backwards. She wanted to scream. He stalked away from her, pulling the blanket from the side of the horse and removing a silver bottle. 'Would you like some water?'

She took it gratefully, taking a drink before handing it back to him. A drop of water escaped from the corner of her lips and before she could catch it, he'd reached out, his fingertip chasing it away then lingering beside her mouth.

She was in a world of trouble.

He took the bottle, had a drink then replaced it. 'Come on.' The words were gruff but she knew why. He wasn't impatient or annoyed. He was fighting himself, trying to get control of how he felt about her and what he wanted. He was fighting the same war he'd been fighting since the night of the masquerade, when they'd learned who they truly were.

It was a war, she realised in a blinding moment of clarity, that they were both destined to lose. Just as passion had overpowered them on that first night, without reason or sense, it would triumph again.

'Do you—?'

Another sentence she didn't—couldn't—finish.

'Do I?'

'Need to tie him up?' She jerked her thumb towards the horse without looking away from Amir. His eyes briefly flicked to the animal, his lips curling when he returned the full force of his attention to Johara.

'No. He will stay nearby.'

A *frisson* of awareness shifted across her spine. 'Because you're the Sheikh and everyone and everything in this kingdom must obey you?'

His brows lifted, amusement and something

far more dangerous flickering in the depths of his eyes. 'Because he is well trained.' He shifted his body weight from one foot to the other, the act bringing him infinitesimally closer. 'And yes, because he obeys me.'

Every feminist bone in her body despaired at the pleasure she took in that—the idea of submitting to this man was sensual and pleasing and answered some archaic desire deep within her. She revolted against it, blinking to clear those desperately unworthy thoughts and forcing herself to step away from him, pretending fascination with the ruins. It was a fascination she shouldn't have needed to pretend. The ruins were beautiful, ancient, endlessly steeped in history and folklore; Johara had longed to see them since she'd first heard about them as a teenager.

Amir clearly knew them well. He guided her through the buildings, or what was left of them, describing what each would have housed. The accommodations, the stables, the hall for dining and the communal courtyard from which announcements were made.

With his words and his knowledge, he brought the ruins to life for Johara. As he spoke, she could see the colours, the people, she could imagine the noise—horses snorting and stomping, people talking, laughing. It was all so vivid.

'I never thought they would be this beautiful,'

she said, shaking her head as he led her across the courtyard and through a narrow opening. A tower stood sentinel over the ruins.

'For security,' he murmured. 'This gave a vantage point in all directions.' The stairs were time-worn, carved into low depressions at the centre of each courtesy of footsteps and sandstorms.

'It's perfectly safe,' he assured her as they reached the top and he pushed open another door to reveal a small opening. The balcony was not large—with the two of them standing there, it left about a metre's space, and there were no guard rails, which meant Johara instinctively stayed close to Amir.

'Do you come out here often?'

'I used to.' The sun was so close to the bottom of the horizon, and the sky was now at its finest. Vibrant pink streaks flew towards them, spectacular against a mauve sky with diamond-like stars beginning to shine.

'Not any more?' She looked towards him.

'I have less time now.'

'Right. The whole sheikh thing.' She banged her palm to her forehead, feigning forgetfulness. 'If I were you, I think I'd come here every day, regardless.'

Her sigh made him smile. 'What do you like about it so much?'

'The history.' She answered automatically. 'The tangible connection to the past. When you described the purpose of each of the buildings I felt generations of people come back to life.'

'And you like history?'

'I like the lessons it can teach us,' she said without missing a beat. 'Nothing we do is new. It's important to remember the way things have played out in the past, otherwise humanity will keep making the same mistakes over and over again.'

He studied her face thoughtfully. 'Such as war?' he prompted.

'Well, yes. Such as war.'

'And yet, regardless of the fact we know what war entails and how badly it always ends, we keep finding ourselves in that state. Perhaps it's simply inherent to human nature to want to fight?'

'And assert our dominance?' She pulled a face. 'I'd like to think we can evolve beyond that.'

'There is a lot of evidence to the contrary.'

'We're in a state of evolution,' she retorted, a smile on her lips.

'And you are a hopeless optimist,' he remembered, and just like that, the first night they'd met was a binding, wrapping around them, making it impossible to forget a similar exchange they'd once shared.

'I'm not really. I think I'm a realist who looks on the bright side wherever possible.'

'Ah.' He made a sound of having been corrected. 'And I'm a realist who doesn't look on the bright side?'

'You're just a hyper-realist.' She smiled at him, an easy smile that morphed into something like a grin and then slowly began to fade from her face as the sun began to drop towards the horizon, so close to disappearing. She angled her face towards it, wondering why she felt as though she'd run a marathon, why her breath felt so tight in her lungs.

'From here, you can see all the way to the mountains in this direction.' He lifted his arm towards the north. She followed and nodded, her throat thick with feeling. 'And in this direction, the palace—though it wasn't there when this was built.'

'No,' she agreed, the words just a croak. The sun was a fireball in the sky, burning close to the horizon. The colours emanating from it were magnificent. Amir's falcon circled overhead and Johara's eyes followed its stately progress, each span of its wings spreading something before her. Magic. Destiny. A sense of fate.

She wrenched her gaze back to Amir's. 'Thank you for bringing me here.'

That same muscle throbbed low in his jaw. 'Don't thank me. My reasons were purely selfish.'

'Oh?' It was just a breathy sound. 'You're not planning on throwing me off the tower, are you?' She strove for lightness, something to alleviate the suffocating tension that was tightening around her.

He shook his head slowly. His hand lifted to her hair, touching it so gently, so reverently, that she pressed her head towards him, craving a deeper touch.

'I wanted to be alone with you, as we were in the maze.'

Her stomach swooped and dropped.

'You were right the other night.'

She didn't say anything.

'I intended to use you as—how did you put it?'

'A scapegoat,' she murmured quickly.

'Yes, a scapegoat.' His smile was laced with self-mockery. 'You were right.'

'I know.' She looked away from him but he lifted his fingers to her chin, gently tilting her face back to his. His fingers moved lower, tracing the pulse point at the base of her neck. He must have been able to feel the frantic racing of it.

'I do want you.'

She didn't say anything.

'But the boundaries of what this is—of what

it can be—are something I have no power to affect.'

Her head felt dizzy. She swayed a little. He put a hand out, wrapping it around her waist, holding her against him. They were bound like that, drawn together, unable to be apart. At least for now.

'The peace is tenuous. And making it last is the most important thing I will ever do in my life. I must make this work—my people deserve my absolute dedication to this cause. If news were to break that something personal was happening between us, you a Qadir and me a Haddad...'

She swallowed. 'We slept together once. No one needs to know.'

His brow creased, his eyes grew serious. 'I'm not talking about then. Right now, this day, standing here with you, I want you, Johara. I want more of you. All of you. While you're here in this country, I want you in my life, my bed, I want you to myself whenever we can manage it. I can offer you nothing beyond this—the decision is yours. Is this enough?'

CHAPTER EIGHT

'IS THIS ENOUGH?'

The sun slipped beyond the horizon, bathing the sky in the most magical, iridescent colours. The beating of the falcon's wings was slow and rhythmic, lulling her even as she felt the urgency of what he was asking. She tried to swallow; her mouth was drier than the desert sands.

There was a small part of her capable of rational thought and it was telling her that no, what he was offering wasn't enough. But it had to be. A little time with Amir was better than nothing; she knew it was temporary but she couldn't muster the strength to object to that—not if the alternative was that they close the door on whatever this was once and for all.

She blinked up at him, the inevitability of this completely breathtaking, and swayed closer. He inhaled deeply, as though breathing her in, and she smiled.

'Yes.' Relief flooded her. It was the right decision.

He made a groaning sound as he dropped his mouth to hers, kissing her even as his hands reached for the bottom of her tunic and pushed at it, lifting it just high enough to expose an inch of midriff. It was like breaking a seal; the moment his fingertips connected with her naked flesh she ached for him in a way that wouldn't be repressed. Her hands pushed at his robes, impatient and hungry, stripping them from his body as he did the same to her, revealing their nakedness simultaneously.

The sun dropped down completely; darkness began to curl through the sky. He drew her to her knees, kneeling opposite, kissing her, his hands wrapping around her as he eased her backwards: carefully, gently. The rooftop wasn't large, there was just space for them to lie together, and little more. He brought his body over hers, his eyes scanning her features, searching for something she couldn't fathom. Or perhaps she could, because she smiled and nodded, in response to his unanswered question, and then pushed up and kissed him, her mouth teasing him, her fingertips playing with the hair at his nape.

He drew his mouth from her lips to her collarbone, lighting little fires beneath her skin everywhere he kissed, his tongue lashing her to the edge of her sanity. She was tipped over the brink when he flicked one of her nipples; she arched her spine in a silent invitation, her fingernails dragging down his back. It reminded her of the way she'd marked him in the maze, making her smile—she lifted up and bit his shoulder, sinking her teeth into the flesh there and laughing as he straightened to fix her with a look that was equal parts smouldering and surprised.

His hands trapped hers, holding them over her head; she was no longer laughing. She couldn't. The power of what they both wanted was almost terrifying. He pushed her legs apart with his knee then kissed her, hard, her body completely trapped by his, her needs driven by him.

'No turning back,' he said into her mouth, pushing the words deep into her soul, where they took hold and filled her with relief. She didn't want to turn back. From the moment she'd discovered who he was, she'd wanted this—come hell or high water.

'No turning back,' she agreed, breaking the kiss just so she could meet his eyes, in the hope he would see the seriousness of her response.

He claimed her mouth as he drove his arousal between her legs and into her feminine core. The relief of welcoming him back brought tears to her eyes. She kissed him with all the fierceness of her desire, lifting her legs and wrapping them around his back, holding him deep inside, allowing her body to glory in his possession. He began to move, hard and fast, as though driven by an ancient tempo that only they could hear.

His body was her master, and hers was his. Beneath the darkening sky, Amir made her his, watching as pleasure exploded through her again and again before giving into his own heady release, filling her with all that he was, holding her to him, their breath racked, their pleasure beyond compare.

Amir lay atop Johara for several minutes after, but it could have been days or months; there on the roof of a tower in the middle of the desert, time had no meaning. They were particles of life in amongst the sand and the history, as utterly a part of the earth as the elements that made this striking, barren landscape what it was.

Johara felt every bit a desert princess, overcome with a sense of her own power. Seeing the effect she had on him—that they had on each other—made her wonder at how they'd been able to resist doing this for as many days as they had!

Her eyes found the stars overhead—the sky had darkened to an inky black now—and she smiled at the thought that the celestial bodies alone had witnessed this coming together. It made it feel all the more powerful and important; all the more predestined.

Eventually, he pushed up onto one elbow, his gaze roaming her face possessively, as if looking for a sign of how she felt. So she smiled, and lifted a hand to cup his cheek, drawing his attention to her eyes. 'That was perfect.'

His features bore a mask of tightness but then he relaxed, smiling, rolling off Johara but simultaneously catching her and bringing her to lie with her head on his chest, his arm wrapped around her. She curled her body to his side, and his hand stroked her hip, his fingers moving with a slowness that could have induced drowsiness. Except Johara wasn't tired; far from it. She felt alive in a thousand and one ways. Her body had caught fire and she wasn't sure those fires would ever be extinguished.

'This is…complicated,' he said with a shake of his head, and then laughed, turning to face her. She saw the same thing in his expression that she felt in her heart. Surrender. This was bigger than them, bigger than the war. It was something neither could fight.

'No.' She shook her head and smiled, pushing up to press her chin to his chest. 'It's the opposite of that—it's so simple.'

He reached out, lacing his fingers through

hers, stroking the back of her hand with his thumb. 'Yes.' He sighed. 'It is also simple.'

She put her head back down, listening to the strong, steady hammering of his heart. All her life she'd been told that the Haddads were the worst of the worst—not to be trusted, not to be seen as anything but the enemy. Yet here she lay listening to Amir Haddad's heart and she knew the truth—it was a good heart. A kind heart. A heart that lived to serve his people.

A heart that would never belong to anyone but his people.

Especially not her—a Qadir.

She pushed those thoughts away. They both knew what they were doing, and what the limitations of this were. That didn't mean she couldn't enjoy it in the moment.

Her fingertips traced the inked words that ran across his chest. 'What does this mean?'

He shifted a little, flicking a glance at his chest, then focussing his attention back on the stars overhead. *'Amor fati,'* he said the words quietly.

'Yes. I love...' she translated with a small frown.

'It's Nietzsche,' he said. 'It means to love one's fate.' He turned towards her, scanning her face as if to read her reaction.

She was contemplative. 'Your fate, as in your role as Sheikh?'

His smile was dismissive. 'Partly, yes. All of it. My parents' death, the duty that put upon me. There was a time when I felt that what was required of me might cripple me. I was only young—fifteen, or sixteen—and I remember riding out here and lying just like this. Well...' a smile lifted his lips at the corners '...not quite like this—there was no woman.'

She smiled back, but didn't say anything; she didn't want him to stop speaking.

'I lay here and looked at the stars and felt as though the sky was falling down on me, suffocating me with its vastness. How could I—a boy completely alone in the world, with no parents, no siblings, only paid advisors—possibly be what was best for the country?'

'It was an enormous responsibility to bear at such a young age,' she said quietly.

'I felt that way *then,*' he responded quietly. 'I now realise that this responsibility was a gift. What a great thing, to be able to lead my people, to rule a country such as this.' He waved his hands towards the sand dunes that rolled away from these ruins.

'Amor fati,' she said simply.

'Yes. I lay here and realised that I was being

self-indulgent. There was no sense wondering if I could be Sheikh. I was. And so I had to be.'

'If it makes any difference, you strike me as a natural at this.'

'Oh?'

She nodded. 'The night we met, before I knew who you were, I knew, somehow, *what* you were.'

'And what is that?'

'A ruler.' Her smile was slow to form. 'You have a natural authority that can't help but convey itself.'

He laughed gruffly. 'I'm used to being obeyed.'

'It's more than that. It's the way you move, the way you speak. I think that your fate chose you.'

'We could also say your uncle chose my fate.'

Her eyes flashed to his and pain sliced through her—brief and sharp. He saw it and shook his head by way of apology. 'I shouldn't have said that.'

'No.' She bit down on her lip. 'But you're right.' Her fingers chased the tattoo, running over the inky black lines. 'He was—is—an extremist. He always has been. He felt my parents were too moderate, that an all-out offensive was called for. He believed that only by destroying Ishkana could Taquul truly prosper. He wanted the war brought to an end once and for all—by any means necessary.'

'He wanted genocide,' Amir said quietly, but

with a ruthless undercurrent to the words. 'And it is best if we do not discuss Johar.' The name was said with disgust.

She nodded. He was right. There was nothing she could ever say that would pardon her uncle's sins; nor did she want to. She judged him as harshly as Amir did.

'I am sorry,' she said quietly.

That drew his gaze, and the look in the depths of his obsidian eyes did something funny to her tummy—tying it in a bundle of knots.

'It was not your fault, Johara.'

He said her name quietly, without a hint of the anger he felt for Johar.

She expelled a soft breath. 'I mean that I'm sorry you had to go through that. The grief...'

He pressed a finger to her nipple and drew an imaginary circle around it. She could barely concentrate. His touch was sending little arrows of need darting beneath her skin.

'Why did you send for me tonight?'

He lowered his mouth, pressing a kiss to the flesh just above her nipple. She shivered.

'I shouldn't have.' He lifted his head to smile. 'I told myself—after the library—that I would stay away from you. But then I saw you looking at me and I knew you felt the inevitability of this.' He lifted a finger, tracing her cheek. 'I knew that if I sent for you and you came, it would be because you didn't care about how forbidden and impossible this is.' He brought his mouth to hers. 'I sent for you because I found myself unable to resist.'

She moaned as he kissed her, her hands seeking his body once more, a new hunger growing inside her. She gave herself to the power of that, falling back against the cool granite of the tower as their bodies became one once more.

'It's best if I leave you at the West Gate.'

They hadn't spoken since leaving the ruins. It was as though each step of the powerful horse brought them closer and closer to the palace and the reality that awaited them. Out there, in the wildness of the desert, nothing had seemed impossible, but the constraints of who they were grew more apparent as the palace loomed into sight.

'Where will you go?'

'I'll take him to the stable yard.'

'You're afraid of being seen with me?'

She felt his harsh intake of breath. 'We discussed this. What we just did has to be kept secret.'

'I know.' She swept her eyes downwards, studying the horse's thick mane, wondering at the cloying sense of tears.

'There are a thousand reasons we cannot let

anyone know what we're doing.' He brought the horse to a step and leaned forward, pressing a hand to the side of her face, drawing her to look at him.

His teeth clenched as he saw the raw emotion on her features.

'Johara...'

'I know. The war. The peace treaty. I'm a Qadir, you're a Haddad.'

'Yes,' he said, gently though, leaning forward and pressing his forehead to hers. 'But it's so much more than that. You are supposed to be marrying Paris. What would the press make of an affair with me while you are all but engaged?'

'I'm not engaged,' she said stiffly.

'In the media's eyes—and I believe your brother's eyes—you are. Your reputation would be damaged beyond repair.'

'This isn't the eighteen hundreds, Amir. No one expects a sacrificial virgin at the altar.'

'No, but you are a princess and people expect *you* to be perfect.'

She pulled away from him, jerking her face in the opposite direction.

'And I suppose you have similar concerns,' she said darkly.

Amir didn't pretend to misunderstand. 'One day I will marry. At present, my kingdom has no heir. But there is no one who would be hurt by our affair.'

'Paris and I are *not* a couple.'

Amir compressed his lips. 'As I said, I believe, in the eyes of your brother, your union is a *fait accompli.*'

'So what I want doesn't matter?'

'It matters. To me, it matters a great deal. I cannot speak on your brother's behalf.'

So measured! So reasonable! She wanted to scream.

And yet, he was right—she'd already felt the pain of being the press's latest object of fascination. For months she'd been hounded after her break up with Matthew. Anyone who'd known either of them had been pressed to give a 'tell all' interview. Private photographs had been found and shared in the articles. The invasion had been unbearable. It had been the catalyst for her departure to America.

Regardless of Paris, having an affair with the Sheikh of Ishkana would be huge news. Her people would hate it. Her brother might never forgive her.

She turned back to face him, regretting the concern she saw on his features, because she'd put it there with her silly reactions.

'You're right.' She nodded firmly. 'I'll go in the West Gate.'

His eyes lingered on her face a moment longer, as if he was reassuring himself before pulling on the reins, starting the horse back on the path.

At the gate, he paused in the midst of a row of pomegranate trees.

'Your schedule is busy tomorrow.'

'I know.'

'I won't see you until the afternoon.'

'At the tour of the *masjid*?'

'Yes, I'll be there too. But we won't be alone.' He cupped her face. 'Tomorrow night, meet me in the forest. Do you remember the way?'

She nodded. 'I think so.'

'Good. Just come to the edges of it. I'll be waiting.'

'What time?'

He thought of his own schedule, and knew he would clear whatever he needed to be available. 'I'll be there from seven. Come when you can.'

Her heart was speeding. Seven o'clock felt like a lifetime away.

He climbed off the horse then reached up and took her hips in his powerful hands, lifting her easily off the back of the stallion. He held her close, and everything that was primal and instinctive stirred to life inside her.

'As soon as you can,' he said with a smile, but

there was a darkness to that—the overpowering need shifting through them.

'I will.'

He kissed her—a light touch of his lips to hers—but it wasn't enough for Johara. She needed more—she didn't want to leave him. She lifted up, wrapping her arms around his neck, deepening the kiss, her body melded to his, and he made a thick noise in his throat as he held her tight to his body, kissing her back with the same hunger before pulling apart, wrenching himself free, breaking what was already becoming something neither could easily control.

They stared at one another for several seconds before a noise had her breaking away from him, moving quickly to the palace wall and pressing against it. He watched her for several beats before swinging onto his horse, pressing himself low to the neck and riding away.

Johara watched him go, her heart racing, her cheeks hurting from the ridiculous smile she couldn't shake.

CHAPTER NINE

IT WAS AN hour into the tour of the *masjid* that Amir began to suspect Johara was a far better actor than he.

She was listening with all of her attention as the *allamah* showed them through the historic place of worship. It was Amir who was struggling to concentrate. He found his eyes straying to Johara when he too should have been listening. He found that he sought her out every few moments, trying to get her to look at him, wanting to see something in her eyes.

What?

Why did he need to look at her so badly?

To know that she didn't regret it.

He compressed his lips and looked away, turning his attention to a piece of art he knew well—a seven-hundred-year-old tapestry weaved from bright and beautiful threads. He moved towards it, as if fascinated by the detail, when in fact he just needed some breathing space.

There was no denying their chemistry; that was clear and mutual. But the danger for them both was real and undeniable. Shouldn't he be protecting her from that by fighting what he felt? For her sake, shouldn't he be stronger?

He closed his eyes, knowing he couldn't. They'd started on this path now and it wasn't in his power to stop.

And yet he could see danger on both sides. He had to at least protect her from discovery. If they could keep this thing secret then when the time came for her to leave, she could continue with her life with no ramifications.

That was what he owed her.

And what about your people? a voice in his head demanded. What would they feel if they knew he'd been intimate with the Princess of Taquul?

He glanced towards her and something in his chest tightened. Yes, she was the Princess of Taquul, but she was so much more. To him, she was simply Johara, but to his people, was it possible she would continue to represent a threat? A reminder of past hatred and violence?

The peace was too important to risk.

Secrecy had to be ensured.

He vowed not to look at her again.

'You're cross with me?' Johara murmured, flicking him an inquiring glance as they walked side by side through the enormous room that led to the large timber doors. It was just the four of them and the *allamah* and Ahmed had moved further ahead.

He jerked his attention to her. 'No.' He looked away again. 'Why would you say that?'

'You're so serious. And trying so hard not to look at me.'

He kept his focus directly ahead. 'To avoid suspicion.'

Her laugh was soft. 'Where's the fun in that?'

And before he could know what she intended, she moved a step closer, her hand brushing against his.

He glared at her. 'Johara.' His voice held a warning.

Her smile was pure teasing. 'Relax. I'm not going to give the game away.' She brushed his hand again. 'But remember, it *is* a game. Try to have a little fun.'

Ahmed turned a moment later. Johara kept walking, no sign of their conversation on her face. 'A crowd has gathered outside. Would you prefer a back entrance?'

Johara looked towards Amir. 'The purpose of my being here is to be seen,' she reminded him. 'We should show a united front.'

He hesitated for some unknown reason, and then nodded. 'Yes. Fine.'

Johara was effortless. He watched as she moved down the stairs, a smile on her face that disguised how she might have felt at being in the heartland of Ishkana so soon after the war had ended. If she held any anger towards his people, she hid it completely.

A woman was calling to her. He watched as she moved closer, but too close! Why didn't she stay back a little? He made a motion to Ahmed, who caught it and signalled to a security guard to intervene, to put some more space between the Princess and the crowd.

But it was too late.

A projectile left the hand of a man near the front of the group. Amir stood frozen to the spot as whatever it was sailed through the air, heading straight for Johara. He swore, began to run, but there wasn't time.

When he reached her, it had hit her square in the chest. The smell was unmistakable. Coffee. Warm, dark coffee was spreading over her white clothing, soaking the fabric, revealing the outline of her breasts. Fury slashed him.

The man was already running but Amir was quick. He reached into the crowd and grabbed him by the collar, pulling him towards through the rope line.

'Your Highness.' Johara's voice was urgent. 'I'm fine. It doesn't matter.'

But Amir barely heard her. He was not a violent man but as he held this person in his grip, he found his other hand forming a fist, and he badly wanted to use it.

'We will take him away,' Ahmed said, moving between Amir and the culprit. The man, to his credit, had the sense to look terrified.

'If you are going to act in this manner, at least stand and face your consequences. Coward,' Amir said angrily, but Ahmed was already pulling the man away, and two security guards had intervened to move Johara into the back of a waiting car.

He followed behind, sliding into the empty seat. Only once they started moving did he turn to her. Her skin was pale, her fingertips were shaking slightly but she was otherwise unharmed.

If there weren't two guards sitting opposite them in the limousine he would have reached across and put a hand over hers. Hell, he would have pulled her onto his lap and kissed her until she forgot anything about such an assault.

'I apologise, Your Highness.'

Her eyes met and held his. 'It wasn't your fault.' She reminded him of what he'd said the night before.

'I assure you, the man will be punished—'

'Don't do that either.' She sighed. 'You said it

yourself. You can tell people we are at peace but you can't make them feel it in their hearts. Why should he be punished for doing something that six months ago he would have been lauded for?'

Amir ground his teeth. 'For the simple reason I have said it is wrong.'

She laughed. 'You are powerful, but not that powerful.'

'You are here as my guest,' he muttered. 'And your safety is my complete responsibility.'

'And?' She fixed him with a level gaze. 'I'm safe, aren't I?'

'It could have been—'

She shook her head. 'It wasn't.' She looked down her front. 'At worst, I'm embarrassed.'

Her phone began to vibrate. She reached into her pocket and pulled it out. Her brother's face stared back at her. She looked at Amir; it was obvious that he'd seen the screen.

She angled away from him a little.

'Mal? This isn't a good…' She frowned. 'That was quick. Yes, I'm fine.'

She was conscious of Amir stiffening in the car beside her.

'As I was just saying to His Majesty Sheikh Amir, it was only a cup of coffee.'

'I don't care.' Malik's voice showed the strength of his feelings. 'What the hell were you doing standing so close to a crowd of wild Ishkani—?'

She glowered at the window. 'How do you know where I was standing?'

'It's already on YouTube.'

'Geez,' she said again, with the shake of her head. 'Thank you, Internet.'

'I want you to come back here.'

Her heart stammered. She looked at Amir unconsciously. 'Nonsense. Because of a bit of coffee?'

'It could have been a bomb. A gun.'

'It wasn't. That wasn't the point the man wanted to make. He's angry. There's anger on both sides. We can't deny people their right to feel those things.'

'Nor should you suffer because of it,' Malik said firmly.

'I'm not suffering.'

'But it—'

'Stop!' She looked at Amir but addressed Malik. 'An inch is as good as a mile, right? It was a coffee. I believe it was a spontaneous act from a man who's suffered through the war. That's all. There's no sense making a mountain out of it.' Her PR mind was spinning over what had happened. 'In fact, if anything, we should make light—include a visit to a coffee house in tomorrow's schedule or something. Show that we have a sense of humour. And under no circumstances will I accept there being any consequences for this man.' She glared at Amir.

'But he—'

She interrupted Malik, waving a hand through the air so the collection of delicate bracelets she wore jangled prettily. 'Yes, yes, he threw a warm coffee cup at me. My clothes will be ruined, and an embarrassing clip is now on the Internet, but so what? Do you know what will happen if we respond too strongly to this?'

Amir was leaning forward a little, captivated by her, wanting to hear what she said—aware that her perspective was one he needed to have.

'We will make the thousands of people who feel that same anger in their hearts want to rise in defence of this poor man. Let's treat his actions with kindness and compassion. No one will expect that, and it will make the forgiveness all the more powerful.'

Amir's eyes drifted to the security guards. They were well trained, not looking at Johara or Amir, but he could see the shift in their faces, the obvious surprise and admiration.

'Now calm down.' She was speaking to her brother but her eyes were on Amir again, and he knew the words were meant for him, too. 'Put your feelings aside, and your concerns for me. I'm fine. Let's speak no more of this.'

* * *

'It is unforgivable.'

Ahmed nodded. 'I'm aware of this. I'll have the police bring charges immediately; he should pay for this.'

Amir was tempted. So tempted. But Johara's words and wisdom were impossible to ignore. He expelled a breath. 'No.' He frowned. 'Have him brought to me here.' Amir thought a moment longer. 'I want to speak to him.'

'To...speak to him?'

Amir flicked his gaze to Ahmed. 'Her Highness has advocated mercy. I'm interested to see if the man deserves such kindness. Bring him here.'

'Your parents were right.'

It was the first thing he said to her when she arrived at the forest, several hours later, a little after seven. They were the words he'd been aching to speak but couldn't until they were alone. Instead, he'd gone back to ignoring her in the limousine, as befitted their perceived relationship.

He drew her towards him, clasping his hands behind her back, his eyes running over her features possessively.

'About what?' The question was breathless. He held her tight.

'You have a gift with people.'

She lowered her lashes, as if embarrassed by the praise.

'I mean it.' He caught her chin, lifting her eyes to his. Something shifted through him, something powerful and elemental. He kissed her; he couldn't help it. 'Were you hurt?'

She shook her head. 'It was just coffee.'

'Hot coffee, and a plastic cup.'

'Yes,' she said, lifting her shoulders. And then, because it was just the two of them, and they were alone, he saw her mask drop, just a fraction. 'I was surprised, and I suppose my feelings were hurt. I was too confident. Everything on this trip has been so easy to date. Your people have been overwhelmingly welcoming, given the circumstances...'

'They've also been accusatory and frosty,' he remarked, pulling away from her, taking her hand and guiding her deeper into the forest.

Her smile was enigmatic. 'Well, yes, at times. But of course they see things from their perspective. Here, I'm the bad guy. In Taquul, that's you.' She lifted her shoulders. 'It's just a matter of perspective.'

'More wisdom.' He squeezed her hand. They moved quickly, both impatient to get to wherever they were going, to be alone.

'I thought you were going to hit him.'

'I wanted to.' He looked down at her.

'I'm glad you didn't.'

'I saw him this afternoon.'

'The man who threw the coffee?' Her brows lifted.

'Yes. Ahmed brought him here, at my request.'

He could feel concern emanating from her in waves. 'Why?'

'To see if you were right.'

'And was I?'

'Yes.'

She expelled a breath. 'People don't generally lash out without cause.'

'No.' He held a vine aloft, waiting for Johara to walk ahead of him. 'His twin brother died in the war. Right at the end.'

Johara's eyes closed in sympathy. 'So recently?'

'Yes.'

'And if peace had been agreed months earlier...'

'He wouldn't have died.' Amir nodded crisply. 'That's why this matters so much. We have to make this work.'

'You will.' She stopped walking to look at him. 'I know Mal is as committed to this as you are. How can peace efforts fail if you're both determined to have this succeed?'

He didn't need to answer. They both knew

there were many things that could unravel the fragile accord. Their relationship was at the top of that list for him. If today had shown him anything it was how close to the surface his people's hostility was.

But he'd looked into the eyes of a man who'd lost so much, who was grieving, and instead of bringing the wrath of his position down on him, he'd spent thirty minutes talking with him. Amir understood grief; he knew it first-hand. He'd listened to the other man and when it became apparent that there had been difficulties accessing his brother's estate—a task he had undertaken for the widow and children—Amir had personally called the parliamentarian who oversaw such matters to ensure it moved smoothly going forward.

Johara had been, in every way, correct. Her wisdom was enviable, so too her grace under literal fire. She would have made an excellent queen.

The thought rocked him to the core. He stopped walking for a second, his eyes fixed straight ahead. They were nearing the edge of the forest, where it gave way to the end of the river. Here, there was a small lake, surrounded on all sides by rock. It was private, held by the palace, the last watercourse between here and the desert.

'What is it, Amir?'

He shook his head, clearing the thought. Johara was intelligent and worldly, but she was certainly not a candidate for the position of his wife. The very idea sent panic along his spine. Anything approaching that would certainly lead to all-out war. Besides, she was the opposite of what he wanted in a wife. When he married, it would be to a woman who was…what? Why couldn't he see that future now? He frowned. Because he was here with Johara—it would be the epitome of rudeness to be thinking of some hypothetical future wife when his lover was at his side.

'I was thinking of Paris,' he substituted, for lack of anything else to say.

'Really?' She frowned. 'Why?'

He began to walk again, forcing a smile to his face. 'I was wondering why your brother is so keen for you to marry him.'

'They've been friends a long time,' she said simply.

'And?'

She laughed. 'Yes, I suppose that's not really an answer.' She tilted her head to the side, considering the question. 'He's a nice guy.'

'The only nice guy in Taquul?'

She flashed him a withering look; he lifted her hand and pressed a kiss to her fingertips.

'Neither of those responses is particularly enlightening.'

'I know,' she sighed. 'Mal is very protective of me.'

Amir didn't want to answer that. He knew that if he said what he felt—that he was glad—she would become defensive. *I don't need him to protect me!* Yet an ancient fibre that ran through Amir liked the idea of someone playing that role in Johara's life, even though he knew she was right—she didn't need it.

'For any reason?' he said instead, and as soon as he'd asked the question, he knew there was more to it.

Her lips pursed, her eyes skittered away. 'You've probably read about it.'

'About what?'

Another sigh. 'Come on, Amir. It was a long time ago.'

'I'm not protecting your feelings, *inti qamar*. I have no idea what you mean.' She looked at him, the term of endearment slipping easily into the sentence. It was what he'd called her in the maze. My moon. Appropriate tonight, when it was glowing overhead, beautiful and enchanting.

'Oh.' She frowned. 'I was with someone before. I was younger, and completely unguarded.

I thought I'd fallen head over heels in love with the guy—so why hide how I felt, right?'

He ignored the prickle of something like jealousy shifting through him. 'Go on.'

Johara nodded. 'We dated for just over a year. It ended badly. The papers got a *lot* of mileage out of it.'

Another burst of emotion, this time one of darkness. 'Newspapers will do that.'

But her expression showed she was lost in thought. 'It was truly terrible. I was twenty-one, and I'd been so sheltered. Worse than that, I honestly thought I loved him. I trusted him.'

Amir's chest tightened. 'He wasn't trustworthy?'

Her laugh lacked humour. 'Not even a little.'

He waited, but not patiently.

'Oh, he didn't cheat on me or anything. But I found out, about six months after our break up, that he'd been selling stories to the gutter press. So many little lies and falsehoods: that we'd had a threesome in Rome—a lie—that I'd secretly fallen pregnant—another lie! All for money!' She shook her head bitterly. 'I would have paid him off, if I'd known money was his motivation.'

Amir reached above them and snapped a twig with more force than was necessary.

'Except I think he also wanted to hurt me,

and, honestly, I think he liked the limelight. When he was my boyfriend, he was followed around by paparazzi, blogs did articles on him.' She shook her head. 'Italian *Vogue* used him as a cover model. But once we broke up, he must have begun to feel irrelevant.'

Amir swore under his breath. 'What a poor excuse for a man.'

She laughed. 'That's pretty much what Mal said.'

'Your brother knew about this?'

'He's the one who discovered the truth.' Her brow furrowed. 'He had the stories investigated.'

'How did he act?'

'He paid Matthew to shut him up.' She grimaced. 'Last I heard, he's living in Australia somewhere.'

'Good riddance.'

'Yeah.' She pressed her teeth to her lower lip. 'So for Malik, he doesn't ever want me to get hurt like that again. And Paris is a great guy, and a good friend of his. Malik trusts him implicitly.'

Something inside Amir bristled. 'But that doesn't mean you should marry him.'

'No,' she agreed softly. 'And yet...'

Amir held his breath.

'This is something we shouldn't discuss.'

He forced himself to sound normal. 'Why not?'

'Because we're sleeping together.'

'And we're both aware that's where this ends. I'm not harbouring a secret desire to marry you,' he said, trying to make it sound as though the very idea was ridiculous.

'I know.' Her voice was quiet. Wounded? Now he felt like a jackass. 'I guess I feel like there's the whole duty thing. Paris is from a great family. Our marriage makes sense. I like him. I don't know if I'd ever trust my own judgement again, when it comes to men, let alone trusting someone *else* after Matthew. Maybe Paris isn't…'

Amir had changed his mind. He couldn't listen to her talk about the prospect of marrying someone else without wanting to burn the world down. He hadn't expected to feel so possessive of her, but he did. He couldn't fight that, or deny it.

'You are a passionate woman, Johara. If you marry, it should be because your passions are aroused, because your heart is caught, and because you know—beyond a doubt—that the man deserves you. Not because he's nice and your brother thinks he's suitable.'

Her lips parted, her eyes lifting to his. 'And is that how you'll choose a wife?'

He shook his head. 'It's different.'

'Why?'

'Because I'm Sheikh. I don't have the luxury of marrying a woman I choose for any reason other than her suitability to rule at my side.'

They stood there on the edge of the forest, so close, eyes locked, hearts beating in unison, the conversation troubling to both for reasons they couldn't fathom.

Distraction came in the form of one of the *juniya* birds. It flew close to Johara's head, drawing her attention, and she followed it beyond the last tree, her eyes catching the water for the first time. She gasped, shaking her head. Stars shone overhead, bathing the still water in little dots of silver.

'What is this place?'

He saw it through her eyes—the large stones that formed walls, creating the feeling of a fortress, the calm water on the edge of the desert, enormous trees that decorated the circumference but left space for the stars to shine.

'My swimming pool.' He grinned, willingly pushing their conversation aside as he pulled on her hand. 'Are you game?'

She flicked a nervous look at him. 'I don't have a bathing costume...'

He drew her closer, pressing his nose to hers. 'Didn't you hear me? This is private...'

Awareness dawned and she laughed, reaching for the bottom of her shirt. 'I see.'

He stepped back as she discarded her clothes, stripping down to her underwear, then removing that scrap of lace, so she was completely naked. He made a growling noise low in his throat, possession firing through him. She took a step forward, her eyes asking a question he answered with a nod. Her fingers caught the fabric of his clothes, lifting them from his body, more slowly than she had her own, so that he wanted to take over, to strip himself naked and pull her against him.

He didn't.

He stood and he waited, his body being stirred to a fever pitch of desire he could barely handle.

Slowly, painstakingly slowly, she undressed him, her fingers grazing his flesh as she went. Her eyes were huge in the moonlight, dark pools every bit as mesmerising as the water beyond them.

'It's beautiful here.' Her voice was thick; he could only jerk his head in agreement.

Her lips moved forward, pressing against his tattoo, and as she did so she whispered the words, *'Amor fati'*. They reached inside him, wrapping around his heart, his soul, the essence of his being.

He loved his fate. He'd worked to love it,

when it had been, at times, the last thing he wanted. His fate was not this woman; she was an aberration, a temporary pleasure—a guilty pleasure. One he found himself utterly power-less to resist.

CHAPTER TEN

'HOW LONG DID you live in New York?'

Johara ran her fingertips over the water. It
was sublime. She'd lost track of how long they'd
been here. An hour? Less? More?

'Almost four years.'

His brows drew together.

'You're surprised?'

He laughed. 'Are you a mind-reader now?'

She pressed her face closer to his. 'Yours is
easy to read.'

'Oh?'

'For me, at least.'

'Ah.' His grin sparked butterflies in her
bloodstream.

'I should have thought your brother would
object.'

She smiled indulgently. 'Mal didn't like the
idea at first.'

She felt Amir stiffen at Johara's use of the
diminutive of Malik's name. 'But you changed
his mind?'

'We came to a compromise.'

Her smile became harder to keep in place. Her eyes shifted away from Amir's.

'And it was?'

'That I should go. For a time.'

Amir's features darkened. 'For a time? You mean until it suited him to have you come back?'

She wanted to defend Malik but, in truth, the terms they'd struck—terms which had, at the time, seemed reasonable—now infuriated her. 'More or less.' She lifted her shoulders. 'I'm a princess of Taquul. My place is in my country.'

'Where do you want to be?'

Her eyes widened. No one had asked her that before.

'Let's pretend you're not a princess,' he said quietly. 'Where would you choose to make your life?'

Johara's heart turned over in her chest. The first answer that sprang to her mind was ludicrous. Too fanciful to say, much less give credit to. She'd spent five days in Ishkana, and it was a country that would never accept or welcome her. Why should she feel such an immense bond to this place? Her eyes ran over Amir's face without her meaning them to. The answer was right in front of her. *Wherever you are.*

Stricken, she tried to smile and pulled away

from him in the water, swimming towards the edge. He came after her.

'You can't answer?'

Oh, she could answer, but the answer would terrify both of them. She bit down on her lip, and strove for a light tone of voice.

'I am what I am, Amir. I'm Johara Qadir, Princess of Taquul, and while I loved everything about New York, I always knew it was temporary. I knew that, one day, he'd ask me to return home and assume the responsibilities that have been mine since birth.'

But Amir was frustrated by that; she could read it in the terse lines of his face.

'Don't pretend that if you had a sister it would be any different,' she teased, surprised she could sound so light when her heart was splintering and cracking.

He frowned. 'I cannot say what it would be like,' he agreed. 'I understand that he wants you back in Taquul. But marrying Paris is part of the agreement, isn't it?'

She dropped her gaze to the water. Tiny ripples moved from her fingertips towards the water's edge. She watched their progress, thinking of how like life that was—a small action could have such far-reaching consequences. 'Yes.' Her eyes swept shut. 'It's what my brother intends for me to do.'

'And what you want? Does it matter?'

'I can say no,' she murmured, meeting his eyes and wishing she hadn't when a feeling of pain and betrayal lanced her. 'He won't force me. If he tried, I'd leave, and I'd leave for good,' she promised. 'The decision is mine.'

Amir pulled her closer, into his arms, staring down at her for several long beats. The sky was silent; even the juniya were quiet in that moment.

'And there was no one in New York?'

Her breath snagged in her throat. 'On the contrary, Manhattan is heavily populated.'

He didn't laugh. His thumb smudged her lower lip, his eyes probing hers. 'You didn't meet anyone that made you want to stay?'

She shook her head. 'There were children. The most beautiful children. I fell in love with each and every one I worked with. I had friends—have friends. But no, there was no man.'

'I find that impossible to believe.'

'Why?'

'Because you're—'

She held her breath, waiting, needing him to finish the sentence.

But he shook his head, a tight smile gripping his lips. 'Four years is a long time.'

She exhaled slowly. 'It is,' she agreed. 'But

Matthew messed me up pretty good.' She lay backwards in the water, and he caught her legs, wrapping them around his waist, holding her there as she floated, staring up at the sky. There was such safety in his hold on her. She felt— whole. Complete. Content. But not for long, because the realisation of those sentiments brought with it a crippling wave of concern.

'Part of what I loved about meeting you was the anonymity. I felt such a connection with you, and all the better because you had no idea I was Johara Qadir.'

'No.' For a moment his voice broke through the serenity of the moment. She remembered his reaction that night, his assurance that if he'd known he would never have acted on those feelings. And none of this would have happened.

'You couldn't sell the story of what we'd done. You couldn't hurt me.'

Silence followed those words, so she began to regret them, and wish she hadn't revealed so much of herself.

But slowly, his hands curled around her back and lifted her from the water, bringing her body against his. His eyes latched to hers.

'I never want to hurt you.'

She swallowed, her throat thick with emotions. 'I know.'

Staring at him, bathed in moonlight, Johara

felt as though every moment of her soul were shifting into alignment. Everything she'd ever been and whatever she was to become were resonating right there; she was her truest, purest form of self in his arms.

'I hate that a man treated you like that.'

'Yes.' She tried to sound crisp and business-like, but the truth was it still hurt. Not Matthew's deeds so much as her own naivety and quickness to trust. She'd gone against her brother's wishes, she'd ignored his warnings, and she'd paid the price.

'I want to show you something tomorrow.'

The change of subject surprised her. She lifted a single brow, waiting for him to continue.

'The gallery, here in the palace. Will you come and see it with me?'

Her stomach looped. 'I'd like to,' she said, truthfully. 'But my schedule is already jam-packed.'

'Your schedule has been revised.'

She stared at him in surprise. 'Revised why?'

'In light of the security concerns today…'

'That was an angry man with a coffee,' she corrected, shaking her head. 'You had no business interfering with the arrangements my state department made.'

'Your safety is my priority.' He lowered his voice. 'As it is theirs—they were also anxious we limit your exposure to uncontrollable elements.'

'You mean people?'

He smiled, but she wasn't amused. Frustration shifted through her.

'Amir, I'm here to do a job. I want to do it.'

'And you can,' he promised. 'The higher profile events are still there. Your schedule has been curtailed, that is all.' He ran his eyes over her face slowly. 'But if you disagree, then have it reinstated.' He lifted his broad shoulders, but he might as well have been pulling on a string that ran right to her heart. She felt it ping and twinge. 'I trust your judgement.'

The string pulled again. Her heart hurt.

I trust your judgement. No one had ever said that to her before.

She lifted a palm to his cheek. 'Thank you for caring.'

His eyes widened and she saw something like shock in the depths of his eyes before he muted it, assuming an expression that was ironic. 'You're my guest in Ishkana. It's my job to care.'

Boundaries. How insistent he'd been on those boundaries, right from the start. He was insisting on them now, just not in so many words.

'I'll defer to you,' she said. 'On this matter only.'

He laughed, shaking his head. 'Heaven forbid you defer on anything else.'

Her own smile came naturally, but she knew what was at the root of her capitulation. A lighter schedule meant she could sneak more time with him. Her time in Taquul was almost at an end. They had to make the most of the days they had left.

'Your Majesty.' Ahmed's expression showed worry. 'It's four in the morning. Where have you been?'

Amir hadn't expected to be discovered returning to the palace. He stared at Ahmed, a frown on his face, wondering for a moment what he should say before realising he didn't have to say anything. He answered to no one.

'Did you want something?'

Ahmed continued to stare at Amir. His hair was wet, and, while he'd pulled his pants on, he'd left his robe off for the walk back to the palace. He had it thrown over one arm now. He'd been too distracted to dress.

'If you're going to insist on monopolising me, then I shall have to think of a form of payback.'

'Oh? What do you have in mind?'

She'd straddled him, taking him deep within her, and leaned over him so her dark hair teased his shoulders. 'What if I told you I have no intention of wearing underwear tomorrow, Amir?'

A smile flicked at his lips as the memory seared his blood. Desire whipped him. It was practically daylight, and still he found he couldn't wait to see her again.

'Yes, sir. There's been an intelligence report. A band of vigilantes is forming in the foothills.'

Amir heard the words with a heavy heart, the statement jolting him back to the present, regretfully pushing all thoughts of Johara and her promise from his mind. 'Well, that didn't take long.'

'No, sir.' Ahmed's voice was similarly weighted.

'Damn it.' Amir dragged a hand through his hair. 'Give me twenty minutes then meet me in my office. Have Zeb join us,' he said, referring to the head of the security agency.

'Yes, sir.'

'Your hair is like a bird's nest,' Athena chastised with a smile. 'What in the world happened?'

Johara smiled, remembering every detail of the night before. 'I went swimming.' The words emerged before she could catch them. Her eyes met Athena's in the mirror. 'Alone. Last night. I found a stream and it was so hot, and no one was around...'

Athena stared at Johara as though she were losing her mind. 'Your Highness...'

Johara sighed, reaching up and putting a hand on Athena's. 'It's fine. No one saw me.'

She could see the fight being waged inside Athena. Their relationship was strange. While they were friends, it was a friendship that existed in a particular way. Athena would never overstep what she considered to be her place, despite the fact Johara often wished she would.

'What is it, Thena?' She pronounced her friend's name 'Thayna', as she always did when she wanted to set aside their professional roles and be simply two women who'd known each other a long time.

Athena's smile, though, showed the conversation was at an end. 'I was just thinking how to style it. A bun will hide the mess.'

'These are your parents?' She stopped walking, staring at the beautifully executed portrait, her eyes lingering on every detail.

'Yes.' At her side, Amir was very still. 'Painted the year of their marriage.'

'She's beautiful.' And she was. The artist had captured something in his mother's features that made Johara feel a tug to the other woman. She shifted her gaze to Amir's, conscious that servants surrounded them so keeping a discreet distance and a cool look pinned to her face. 'You have her eyes.'

He returned her look but it was futile. It didn't matter how cool either of them attempted to appear, heat sparked from him to her, making her fingertips tingle with an impulse to reach out and touch. She ached to drag her teeth across his collarbone, to flick her tongue in the indentation of his clavicle, to run her fingertips up his sides until he grabbed her and pinned her to the wall...

Her cheeks flushed, and she knew he recognised it because his attention shifted lower in her face and a mocking smile crept over his mouth—mocking himself or her, she didn't know.

She turned away from him, moving a little further down the hallway, her gaze sliding across the next painting—another couple. 'My grandparents,' he supplied. The next had her feet stilling, to study it properly.

'It's you.'

It jolted him—the painting had been done when he was only a small boy. 'How can you tell?'

'Your eyes,' she said seriously. 'And your smile.'

Ahmed had moved closer without either of them realising, and caught her observation, a small frown on his face. 'I beg your pardon, Your Majesty.' He addressed Amir alone.

'What is it?' Amir's impatience was obvious.

'There's an update, on the matter we discussed this morning. Zeb has the information. He's waiting in your office.'

Amir's brow creased in consternation but he

nodded, turning back to Johara. 'I have to deal with this.'

Disappointment crested inside her. Perhaps Amir sensed it because he lowered his voice, though Ahmed stood at his elbow. 'I won't be long.'

It was too obvious. Heat sparked in Johara's cheeks. She looked away, nodding with what she hoped appeared disinterest. 'It's no bother, Your Majesty. I have plenty here with which to occupy myself.'

Amir didn't stay a moment longer than necessary. He turned on his heel and stalked down the corridor. Johara watched until he'd turned a corner, before realising that Ahmed was still there, his eyes intent on her face.

She forced a polite smile. 'The artwork here is first class.'

'Yes, madam.'

Frosty. Disapproving. She turned away from him, telling herself she didn't care. She continued to tour the gallery, each painting deserving far more attention than she gave it. She couldn't focus on anything other than Amir.

'My mother used to play the piano,' Amir said quietly. 'She was very good. When I was a child, I would listen to her for hours.'

Johara reached for another grape, grateful that they were—finally—alone. It had taken a heck of a lot of logistics but they'd managed to

find a way to give all of their servants the slip,
so that they could now sit, just the two of them,
in his beautiful private hall that he'd brought her
to the first morning she'd arrived. The morning
he'd asked if she was pregnant. How much had
happened since then!

'Do you play?'

He shook his head. 'No. I think her musical-
ity escaped me.'

'Music can be taught,' she pointed out.

'The techniques can be, but not the passion
and the instinct.'

Johara smiled. 'Remind me never to play if
you're in attendance.'

'You play piano?'

'Yes.' She reached for another grape, but before she could pluck it from the vine he caught it
and held it to her mouth instead, his eyes probing hers as he pushed it between her lips. Passion and desire were like flames, licking at the
soles of her feet.

'Strangely, it was one of the things I excelled at.'

'Your dyslexia didn't make it difficult for you
to read music?'

'Impossible.' She laughed. 'But I hear something and can play it.'

'I'm impressed.'

'Don't be.'

He lifted another grape to her mouth.

'It's just the way my brain is wired.'

'I want to hear you play.'

She leaned closer, pressing a kiss to the tip of his nose. 'And yet, I just said I won't play for you.'

'And what if I ordered you to?' His voice was mock-demanding.

She laughed. 'You and what army?'

He moved closer, grabbing her wrists, pinning them above her head as he used his body to press her backwards. 'Haven't you heard? I'm King of all I survey.'

'Including me?' she asked, breathless, lying on her back with Amir on top of her, the weight of him so pleasing, so addictive.

'Definitely you.'

'Ah, but I'm not one of your subjects,' she reminded him. 'I'm the enemy.'

He stared at her, his look serious. 'Not my enemy.'

It was strangely uplifting, but she didn't want to analyse the meaning behind his statement, because it would surely lead to disappointment. She kept her voice amused.

'My allegiance has to be earned.'

He smiled lazily, releasing one hand while keeping her wrists pinned easily in the other. He traced a line down her body, over her breasts, finding the peaks of her nipples and circling them before running his hand lower, and lower still, to capture the fabric at the bottom of the long dress she wore.

'I can think of one way to ensure loyalty.'

'Oh?'

'Let me see, first, if you are a lady of honour.'

She laughed. 'A what?'

'If you are true to your word.'

'Oh!' Heat stained her cheeks. She held her breath as his fingers crept up the satiny skin of her inner thigh and found what he was looking for—nakedness. She had gone without underpants for him. And she'd hoped he'd remembered her parting statement, and that the thought had driven him as wild as it had her.

His answer was everything she'd hoped for.

'Well?' she asked huskily.

'Just as promised.' He spoke with reverence. Their eyes met and something shifted inside her heart.

His dark head dipped down, his tongue stirring her to a fever pitch of longing, making her ache for him, reminding her of the maze, of everything they'd shared together since, of everything they were. Pleasure, passion, power; her blood was exploding with needs, her pulse too fast to be contained. She pushed up, needing him, wanting more than he could offer, craving the satisfaction she knew it was within his grasp to give. His mouth moved faster and she shattered, her fingertips driving through his hair, her mouth capable of shaping only two syllables: *Am* and *Ir*. Over and over and over she cried his name, as though it were an invocation that could ward off what they both knew was coming.

But she refused to think of the future, about what would happen in two days' time, when her tour was at an end and the flight took her back over the mountains to Taquul, and the future that was waiting for her.

She couldn't think about that. Not when there was this pleasure to be relished and enjoyed.

He knew they needed to move, to leave this sanctuary. He was Sheikh and, despite the fact he answered to no one, he couldn't simply disappear for hours at a time without arousing suspicion. His absence would be noticed. So too, he imagined, would hers.

But the weight of her head on his chest was so pleasant. Just for a little while longer, he wanted to keep the doors to this room shut, to lie as they were: naked on the scatter pillows, the heady fragrance of trees and flowers and the sound of flowing water creating their own world and atmosphere. It was a *masjid* first and foremost and here he felt that he was worshipping Johara as she deserved to be worshipped.

'Will you come to my room tonight?'

The question surprised him—he hadn't intended to ask it, but he didn't regret it.

'Sure.' Her voice, though, was teasing. 'I'll just let your guards know I'm popping in for a quick roll in your bed. That won't raise any eyebrows whatsoever.'

He laughed, shifting so he could see her face. 'There's a secret way.'

She met his gaze. 'Into your room?'

'Yes.'

'Why?' And then, realisation dawned. 'For exactly this purpose.'

Another laugh. 'Yes.'

'So you…sneak lovers in…regularly?'

He heard her hurt and wondered at his body's response to it. He wanted to draw her into his arms and tell her she had nothing to be jealous of. He'd never been with a woman like her. He doubted he ever would be again.

'No, Johara. Never.'

'Oh. Then why…?'

'Because my room has been the Sheikh's room for many hundreds of years.' He lifted his broad shoulders. 'And whichever palace concubine my predecessors decided to amuse themselves with would arrive via a secret tunnel.'

Her jaw dropped. 'You're not serious.'

Her innocence made it impossible not to smile. 'Perfectly.'

'But...'

'But?'

'Well, it's a security risk, for one,' she huffed.

'It is not a corridor anyone knows about.'

'Want to bet?'

He arched a brow, waiting for her to continue.

'It seems to me like the kind of thing your enemies would pay a lot of money to learn about.'

'The palace is guarded like a fortress.'

'I know that.'

'It's safe.'

'I know that too.' She gnawed on her lower lip, her eyes clouded, but after a moment she sighed, surrendering despite her first response. 'Well? How do I find it?'

CHAPTER ELEVEN

'THIS PLACE IS...'

She looked around, wishing she didn't find the room so incredibly sumptuous and sensual. 'I mean...'

His smile was sardonic. 'Yes?' But he knew how she felt. Shirtless, wearing only a pair of slim-fitting black trousers, he prowled towards her, capitalising on the overwhelm a space such as this had given her.

The carpets were a deep red in colour, the furnishing a similar colour, velvet, with gold details. There were chairs but in the middle of the space, making it very obvious exactly what the room was to be used for, was the most enormous bed Johara had seen. It could easily accommodate ten people.

Her mouth felt dry as she stepped towards it, studying it with a curiosity she couldn't resist.

'What's that?' She ran her finger over an ornate brass hook that hung in the centre of the bed's head.

'For handcuffs.'

She spun around to face him, oddly guilty. 'Handcuffs?' The question squeaked out of her.

He prowled closer, and the nearer he got, the faster her pulse went. She bit down on her lip as he grabbed her wrists, rubbing his thumb over them. 'Or rope. Or silk. Whatever your preference.'

Her eyes moved back to the bed, as desire ran the length of her spine.

'Does it tempt you?'

She shivered quite openly now, lifting her eyes to his, uncertainty in their depths. Yes, she wanted to say. It tempted her—a lot. But only with him! It was a fantasy she'd never had before—never even thought to have. But with Amir, the idea of being tied up and made love to was, perhaps, the most intoxicating thing she'd ever contemplated.

So she clung to outrage instead, because she was aware of how dangerous her supplication had become, how completely she'd surrendered to Amir and his ways.

'I just can't believe there's a place like this in your palace. A harem!'

His smile showed he knew exactly how she felt, and why she was intent on denying it.

'It hasn't been used since my great-grandfather's reign.'

She looked away, her eyes betraying her and straying to the hook once more, her nipples straining against the silk fabric of her bra.

She was fighting a losing battle.

'So what do you do when you're dating a woman?' she prompted, needing to focus on something other than this overtly sexual room, and the hook that would accommodate handcuffs just perfectly.

He tilted his head, waiting for her to continue. 'Are you asking if I bring women here?' he prompted, gesturing to the bed.

'God, no.' She shook her head urgently, not wanting *that* image in her mind. 'I just meant... do you date, publicly? Can women come to your room?'

'I can do whatever I want,' he said gently. 'I'm Sheikh.' He pressed a finger to her chin, lifting her face to his. 'It is for you that we must be secret about this—and for the sake of the peace treaty.'

She nodded. 'So if I were just some woman you'd met, you'd have me delivered to your room whenever it suited?'

His laugh was little more than a growl. 'You make it sound so archaic. So one-sided. If you were just a woman I'd met,' he corrected, 'I would invite you for dinner. We would share a meal and then I would ask you if you wanted to come to my room. The choice would be—as it is now—yours.'

Her heart turned over in her chest. She had the suspicion she was being combative and she didn't know why. Something was needling her, making her frustrated and wanting to lash out.

'I'm sorry,' she said truthfully, lifting her fingers to his chest and pressing them there. 'I don't know why I'm acting like this. I just didn't expect this room to be so—'

'Confronting?' he suggested. Then, 'Unpalatable.'

She shook her head, not meeting his eyes. 'Palatable,' she corrected, so quietly it was barely a whisper.

In response, he pulled her hard against him, and before she could draw breath he was kissing her as though everything they cared for in this life depended on it. Her body moulded to his like it was designed to fit—two pieces carved from the same marble. She felt his heart racing in time with hers, thudding where hers was frantic, a baritone to her soprano.

Time and space swirled away, concepts far in the distance, as he stooped down and lifted her easily, kissing her as he cradled her against his chest, carrying her through this room and into a corridor that was wide but dimly lit. She felt safe. She felt whole.

She relaxed completely, a beautiful heaviness spreading through her limbs. When they entered his room, she spared it only a cursory glimpse, and took in barely any of the details. It was similar to the suite she'd been provided with, but larger and more elaborate. It was also quite spartan. Where hers was filled with luxurious touches, his had been pared back. The mosaics on the floor were beautiful, but there was no art here. Just white walls, giving the windows all the ability to shine, with their view of the desert. Or, as it was now, of the night sky beyond.

He placed her gently onto the bed then stood, looking at her, his eyes showing a thousand and one things even when he said nothing.

Johara smiled and reached for him—her instincts driving her—and he came, joining her in the bed, sweeping her into his arms once more and kissing her until breathing became an absolute afterthought.

'You don't have to do this, sir.'

'I want to.' Twelve-year-old Amir fixed his parents' servant with a look from the depths of his soul. It was a look of purpose and determination. It was a look that hid the pain tearing him into a thousand little pieces.

'I have identified their bodies, for security purposes,' Ahmed reminded Amir softly, putting a hand on Amir's shoulder. His touch was kindly meant; it was then Amir remembered Ahmed had children of his own, not too far apart in age from Amir.

'I want to see them.'

He spoke with a steely resonance, and it gripped his heart. There was much uncertainty. In the hours since his parents' death, he'd had to grapple with the change in his circumstances, the expectations upon him. He felt deeply but showed nothing. He was a leader. People looked to him.

'Amir,' Ahmed sighed. 'No child should have to see this.'

He drew himself to his full height. 'I said I want to see them.'

It was enough. Even Ahmed wouldn't argue with the Sheikh of Ishkana—for long.

'Yes, sir.' He sighed wearily, hesitated a moment then turned. 'This way.'

The corridor was dimly lit but muffled noise was everywhere. The palace had woken. The country had woken. News had spread like wildfire.

They were dead.

At the door to the tomb where their bodies had been brought to lie, Amir allowed himself the briefest moment of hesitation, to steel himself, and then stepped inside.

Three people were within. Lifelong servants. People who felt his parents' loss as keenly as he, who grieved with the same strength he did.

'Leave me,' he commanded, his eyes falling to his father's face first. He didn't look to see that he'd been obeyed. He knew that he had been. Only Ahmed remained, impervious perhaps to the Sheikh's commands, or perhaps knowing that, despite the appearance of strength, a twelve-year-old boy could not look upon his parents' crumpled bodies and feel nothing.

He kneeled beside his father, taking his hand, holding it, pressing his face to it, praying for strength and guidance. He moved to his mother next, and it was the sight of her that made a thick sob roll through his chest.

She looked asleep. Beautiful. Peaceful. He put his hands on either side of her face, as though willing her to wake up, but she didn't.

It was the worst thing he'd had to do, but seeing his parents like that became the cornerstone of his being.

The war had killed them. Taquul had killed them. The Qadirs...

He woke with a start, his heart heavy, a strange sense of claustrophobia and grief pressing against him, before realising he wasn't alone.

He pushed the sheets back, staring at Johara

in complete confusion. It took him a second to remember who she was, and then it all came flooding back to him—their affair, their intimacy, the way he'd started to think of her and smile at the strangest of times.

What the hell was he doing? His parents' visage was so fresh in his mind, the hatred he'd felt that night—and here he was, with a Qadir…

No. Not a Qadir. Johara.

Her name was like an incantation. It relaxed him, pulling him back to the present, reminding him of everything they'd shared in the past week.

She was a Qadir, but she was so much more than that. When he looked at her, he no longer saw her family, her place in the Taquul royal lineage, her birthright; when he said her name he saw only her, not the uncle for whom she'd been named, the uncle who had orchestrated his parents' murder.

But guilt followed that realisation. He'd promised his parents' dead bodies he would never forget. He'd promised them he would hate the enemy for ever, and here he was, seeking comfort in Johara's arms, craving her in a way he should have been fighting against.

He moved to the windows, the ancient desert a sight that comforted him and anchored him, reminding him who he was. He breathed in its acrid air, letting it permeate his lungs. He was a Haddad. He was of this country, this kingdom, he served the people of Ishkana and nothing would change that.

What he and Johara were doing was… He turned towards the bed, her sleeping body making him frown. He couldn't describe how he felt about her, and this. He knew only that there was a greater danger here than he'd ever imagined.

A knock sounded at the door—loud and imperative. Amir saw that it disturbed Johara and winced, crossing to the door quickly, grabbing shorts as he went and pulling them on. With one quick look over his shoulder, he pulled it inwards. Ahmed stood there, but he was not alone. Zeb, and several guards, were at his back.

Amir pulled the door shut behind himself, shielding his bed and lover from view before consulting his wristwatch. It was almost four. Only something serious would have brought anyone—particularly this contingent of men—to his room at this hour.

'What is it?'

Ahmed nodded. 'There's been an attack.'

Amir tensed. 'Where?'

'In the *malani* provinces.'

His eyes swept shut. Anger sparked inside him. 'How many?'

'Two confirmed dead so far.'

He swore. 'Insurgents?'

Ahmed looked towards Zeb. 'Taquul insurgents,' he said quietly. 'They set off a bomb outside a nightclub.'

Many times in his life had he been told news such as this. He braced for the inevitable information. 'How bad?'

'It's an emerging situation. The damage is being assessed.'

'Whose bomb?'

'That's not clear,' Zeb murmured. 'It has the markings of a state device, though the timing…'

'Yes.' Unconsciously, he looked over his shoulder. It was impossible to believe anyone in Malik's military would be foolish enough to launch an attack while Johara was deep in Ishkana.

'What scale are we talking?'

Ahmed winced. 'It's bad, sir. A building's collapsed.'

Amir swore.

'I've put the border forces on alert.'

Amir stiffened. It was protocol. Zeb had done the right thing, and yet the familiarity of all this hit him like a stone in the gut. Just like that, he could see the peace evaporating.

'We need more information.'

'Sir?' Ahmed's brows were furrowed.

'Was this the act of a rogue military com-

mander, or the insurgents in the mountain
ranges looking to profit from ongoing unease
between our people, or a state-sanctioned skir-
mish in disputed land? We need to understand
what the hell happened and why, before we respond.'

'But you will have to respond,' Zeb insisted.
'We don't have all the details yet but this was
a vicious peace-time attack. Your people will
expect—'

'My people want peace,' Amir said quietly,
thinking of the sadness he'd seen in the eyes of
the man who'd thrown coffee at Johara. 'Not a
knee-jerk retaliation that springs us back into
the war.'

Silence met the statement.

'The Princess—' Zeb's expression was un-
easy. He looked to Ahmed before continuing.
'She would be a good bargaining chip. To ensure Malik apologises, takes responsibility...'

Amir felt a surge of disgust and then rage.
'Even if he had nothing to do with it?'

'I find it hard to believe an attack of this kind
could occur without his involvement.'

'This is what we will discover. But in the
meantime Her Highness remains our honoured
guest. No one is to speak to her of this, to touch
her, to even think of using her in any way. Understood?'

Zeb frowned. 'It is my job to advise you on the best military strategies…'

'Fine. You've advised me.'

'The death toll could be in the hundreds. You must act, sir. I have the eleventh division mobilised. They could retake one of our strongholds in the mountains—'

'No.' He shook his head, then in a tone designed to placate, 'It's too soon.'

'Too soon? The destruction. The inevitable death count—'

'We are no longer at war.'

'What is this if not an act of war?' Zeb pushed with obvious impatience.

Amir fixed him with a stare that was designed to strike fear into the other man. It worked. Contrition overtook his expression. While Amir allowed—and appreciated—a lot of latitude from his advisors, he remained the ultimate power holder.

'We don't have enough information to know yet.'

'But if it was state-sanctioned?'

Amir considered that. He had met with Malik and seen in his eyes the same desire for peace that lived in Amir's heart. They both wanted this, for their people. 'We'll discuss that if we come to it.'

'And you'll respond accordingly?'

Amir compressed his lips, not inclined to answer that without having more of an idea as to the circumstances of the attack.

'The Princess should be held until we know,' Zeb pushed. 'Detain her, show our people that we're not feeding our enemies cake and wine...'

'She is not the enemy,' Amir said cuttingly. 'And I have already told you—no one is to bring her into this.'

'She is in it, though,' Ahmed said gently. 'Her presence alone requires some kind of action.'

Ahmed's words reached inside Amir and shook him, forced him to see clearly the tenuousness of Johara's place here in the kingdom. He had come to know her, beyond the fact she was a Qadir and a princess of Taquul, but why should he expect his people to feel as he did? She could easily become a focus for anger and revenge. His gut rolled with a burst of nausea; his skin felt hot and cold all over.

He turned back to the men. 'I want a meeting in the tactical rooms. Fifteen minutes. Discover what you can in the meantime. I need answers. And I want to speak to Malik Qadir. Arrange that as soon as possible, Zeb.' His eyes met Ahmed's. Something passed between them. Understanding. Agreement. 'Let me be clear here—my goal is to maintain the peace.' He softened his tone. 'For too long we have answered violence with violence; I understand your instincts now are to do the same. But that will only perpetuate what we've always known. The fight for peace will be won with diplomacy, not military force.'

He paused, knowing what he had to do and hating the necessity of it. But for her safety… to prevent anything ever happening to her as had happened to his parents? An image of his mother's face filled his mind, as she'd been the last time he'd seen her, in the tombs beneath the palace. Fear hardened into resolve. Johara would be protected at all costs.

'Johara Qadir will leave the country immediately.' He faced Zeb. 'Her safe passage is the most important job you will have tonight, Zeb. If anything happens to her—'

'I know. It will inevitably renew the war.'

Amir waited until they were gone before pushing the door to his room open. Johara was awake now, looking at him, her eyes huge and hair tousled. He wasn't sure what she'd heard, but it was clear she knew something was amiss.

She stood as he walked towards the bed, her nakedness taking his breath away even then.

'Something's wrong?'

He contemplated not telling her. He contemplated saying nothing, but she deserved to know.

Besides, her brother would undoubtedly contact her imminently.

'Yes.'

'What is it?'

He ground his teeth together, moving towards her. 'There was an attack. A Taquul bomb in one of the northern towns.'

Her features showed surprise and then sorrow. 'You said this would happen.'

'Yes, but I had hoped...' He shook his head. He hadn't, really. He'd known that peace was a Sisyphean task, yet still he'd pushed for it, worked towards it, knowing his people deserved at least a chance. He still believed that. For their sake, he had to quell this, ensure it didn't form the beginning of more conflict. But the attitude of his chief military advisor showed what a battle he was waging—even within his own government.

'Was anyone hurt?'

'Yes.'

'Killed?'

'The exact number is unknown but we expect the count to be high.' She dipped her head forward, and he knew she felt as he did—sorrow. Futility. Anger.

'You have to go.'

She nodded, looking around for her clothes.

'Yes. I shouldn't have fallen asleep. What can I do?'

He stared at her, committing everything about her to memory. He could never see her again. These last few days had been something he could never put into words, but it had to end. She wasn't simply a woman with whom he could enjoy a no-strings affair. He wanted her too selfishly. In another day or two, he wouldn't be able to relinquish her. It had to be now. To his people, and his government, she would always be the enemy. He was putting her at risk every minute he kept her here.

'How can I help?'

Her words were some kind of balm. No one had offered him help—and so simply—all his life. But he pushed the offer aside. 'You misunderstand, Johara. You need to leave Ishkana. I have arranged your transport. You are to leave now, in the dead of night, before the country has awoken to this news.'

Her mouth dropped open.

'That's… No.'

Another surprise. People didn't say 'no' to him. 'You misunderstand me again. I'm not asking you to leave.'

Her eyes narrowed. 'You're ordering me?'

He expelled a sigh, moving across the room and pulling out some clothes. He understood her resentment of that—all her life she'd been ordered around and yet she deserved so much better. He didn't want to be just another person who sought to control her. 'I'm telling you what is going to happen. You cannot be here if war breaks out. The risk to you is too great.'

'War won't break out. My brother and you will work together to prevent that from happening.'

'We don't know yet that this bomb wasn't detonated with your brother's permission.'

She gasped. 'You can't seriously think—'

He shook his head. 'No.' He frowned. 'But war with Taquul is familiar.'

'All the more reason for us to challenge that assumption.'

He shook his head with frustration. Why wouldn't she understand? 'There are powerful members of my government already demanding retribution.'

'You can't do that.'

He ground his teeth together. 'I have to do what is best for my country.'

'And that's peace. We both know that.'

'Yes, Johara, but peace may not be possible.'

She shook her head. 'I refuse to believe that. Let me stay here with you, standing by your side showing that we are committed to a peaceful outcome.'

The image she created was vibrant but impossible. Zeb's response had shown him that. *Detain her.* A fierce reaction resonated along his spine. 'Your place is in Taquul with your people.'

Her eyes sparked with anger. 'Can't you see that's what's wrong with all this? *Your* people. *My* people. They're all damned people, living side by side. Isn't this peace about breaking down barriers, Amir? Wasn't that the purpose of my being here?'

His heart had kicked up a notch. He dragged trousers over his boxers without looking away from her. 'This changes things.'

'It doesn't have to.' She moved towards him with urgency. 'You said, from the outset, there would be difficulties. This is one of them. Are you truly intending to fall at the first hurdle?'

'No.' He reached for a shirt. 'But having you here complicates matters. You have to leave.'

'Why? For whom does it complicate anything?'

'You represent something my people have been taught to hate, and also fear.'

'Me?' She dug her fingers into the space between her breasts; his gut twisted at her look of obvious disbelief. 'I'm just one woman, a woman who's here with an open heart and mind, wanting to improve relations. Your people will see that—just don't push me away. Let me stay. Show your citizens that you and I are both invested in the peace process, that we believe it will succeed...'

'And what if Malik and I cannot agree on this? What if war is inevitable? You think my military will not expect me to keep you as a prisoner?'

She gasped. 'You would never do that.'

'No.' He dragged a hand through his hair, frowning. 'Of course I wouldn't, and that's the problem. You compromise me. This, what we've been doing, has made me forget.' He softened his tone, moving closer. 'But I can't forget.' He lifted a hand to her cheek, touching her for what he knew would be the last time. 'We created a perfect void, you and I. A magical space removed from anything and anyone else. But nothing about this works when the world intrudes. The reality of who we are and what our countries require of us is there, banging at the door. Wake up and hear it, Johara. This has to end and you need to leave.'

He felt her shiver, her body trembling against his hand. 'You're wrong.'

He took a step back. 'This was wrong. I thought we could separate what we were doing from the circumstances of who we are, but I never will. We stand on the brink of war once more. Your people. My people. You, and me. You are a Qadir.'

She shook her head, tears filling her eyes, so he felt pain throb low in his gut. He angled his face away for a moment, unable to see her cry.

'Is that all I am to you?'

He closed his heart against her hurt. 'No. But it's the part of you I have to focus on.'

Silence hung between them, heavy and accusatory. He fixed her with a determined gaze.

'I promise that I will protect you with my dying breath but even that isn't enough to guarantee your safety. I have forbidden my military commander from using you as a pawn in this, but I cannot control this to my satisfaction. You are at risk every minute you remain here, Jo.' The diminutive of her name slipped out in his need to convince her.

'I'm not afraid,' she insisted, her eyes showing fierceness.

'You should be.' He blinked and saw his parents' bodies. His blood turned to ice. 'I will not have your death on my conscience.'

'Then let me absolve you of that. I'm choosing to stay—this isn't your responsibility.'

But she would always be his responsibility. It was inevitable. He didn't want the burden of protecting her; he couldn't lose her because of his selfish desire to have her at his side.

Johara brushed a hand through her dark hair, drawing his attention to her face. 'I won't leave; not now. My visit is scheduled to end tomorrow. Let me stay until then, keep to my schedule. Please, Amir. We cannot capitulate to what's likely to be a few rogues. Why can't you see that? It's exactly what they want! Surely this attack was designed in the hope of disturbing the peace—'

He held a hand in the air to silence her, his blood slamming through his body. 'And what better way to disturb the peace than to harm you? You think that even if you stayed I would ever allow you to keep to your schedule? To leave the palace when the mood is like this? No, Johara.' He refused to soften even when faced with her obvious hurt. 'The night we met, I thought you idealistic. But you are also naïve. You have been sheltered, to some extent, from the ravages of this war. You do not understand the lengths men will go to—'

'How dare you?' She glared at him down the length of her nose. 'How dare you speak to me as though I am—' she stopped abruptly, her face filled with torment '—stupid?' she finished on a sob, pressing her palms to her eyes.

He stood perfectly still, because if he moved, even a little bit, he knew he would crumble altogether. He wanted to cross to her and pull her to him, to wrap his arms around her and hold her tight, to kiss her until this all faded away into nothingness. To tell her that whoever had told her she was stupid because of her dyslexia was mad, because she was the smartest, most courageous person he'd ever known. But he would not weaken. She needed him to be strong; his country needed him to be strong.

Her eyes narrowed, her lower lip trembling, but when she spoke it was in a tone that was pure steel. 'You think you're the only one who's watched his country suffer at the hands of the enemy? I know what we've done to each other! I've lived it, too! That's why we need to stop it. Work together—'

'As your brother and I will do,' he said, determined to turn her away. 'If this was a rogue attack from the mountain people then we will work together to—reason with them and understand them, just as you urged me to understand the man who threw coffee at you. They have played their part in this war and perhaps they have motives we don't comprehend. You've made me see that, Jo. You've changed how I view conflict, people, war. You've changed me.' The admission cost him. It emerged thick and throaty, dark with his emotions.

He paused, bracing himself for what he needed her to know. 'You cannot remain. You are a liability.' He knew he had to be firm, harsh, to get her to see sense. Feeling as though he were dropping off the edge of a cliff, he spun away from her. 'And you're a distraction I don't want, Johara. I need you to go now.'

CHAPTER TWELVE

'YOU'RE A DISTRACTION *I don't want, Johara. I need you to go now.*'

She stared at his back, his intractable words beating her in the chest. Her eyes swept shut; she struggled to breathe. Hearing these things at any time would have been difficult, but naked in his room, she felt vulnerable and exposed, disbelieving too, as though what he was saying went against everything they'd become.

'The fate of my country hangs in the balance. Of course I can't just run away from that.' She looked around for her clothes, and finally saw them discarded near the foot of the bed. She stalked towards them, scooping them up and pulling her pants on quickly. Her fingers shook, making it difficult to clasp her bra into place. 'And you don't know me at all if you think I'm the kind of person who would quit at the first roadblock.'

'Then do what you must in the bounds of

Taquul but you will leave Ishkana, and leave now, before the kingdom awakes to this news.'

'And they'll think I've deserted them! They'll think my opinion of the peace is fragile when it's not! I believe in this peace as much as I believe in this—what you and I share.'

His eyes closed for a moment, as though he was physically rejecting that sentiment. 'They will be far more concerned with whether or not the war is about to break out again.'

'You're making a mistake.' She knew that to be the case. Every cell in her body was screaming at her in violent protest. Leaving was wrong. Not just Ishkana, but Amir. All week she'd braced herself for the necessity of that, and she'd known it would be hard, but, seeing him with the weight of the world on his shoulders, she finally understood what had been happening to them. Ever since that night in the maze.

She lifted a hand to her mouth, smothering a gasp and turning her back on him while she analysed her head, her heart, everything she was feeling.

It was a secret affair, one they'd agreed would have clear-cut boundaries, but Johara's heart…it hadn't realised. Not really. She'd fallen in love with him, with all of herself. The desert sky was still an inky black, the stars overhead sparkling, though now it was with a look of mischief. They'd known what they were doing in the maze, contriving for these two people to see one another and give into that cataclysmic desire. Qadirs and Haddads, unbeknownst, hidden, lovers.

At the very edge of the horizon, where sand met sky, whispers of purple were radiating like flames, promising the break of a new day. Soon it would spread, licking upwards, covering the heavens in colour, and then it would begin. How they acted on this day would determine so much.

She spun back to face Amir. His back was still turned. The sight of him like that, closed off to her, sparked a thousand emotions in her gut. Something inside her snapped, but underneath it all was the wonderment of her realisation.

'What if I stayed?' she said quietly, moving towards him, circumnavigating his frame so they were toe to toe, eyes clashing.

'I won't allow it, and nor will your brother.'

Anger exploded in her gut. 'Neither of you can control me,' she said fiercely.

'This isn't about control. It's about your safety.'

'You're saying you can't keep me safe until this is over?' she challenged him, so close she could feel the exhalations as he worked to control his temper.

'I'm saying your safety would become all I could think of,' he contradicted, putting his hands on her shoulders. 'And I need to focus on *this*—the country—with all of my attention. In Taquul, you will be safe.'

'Maybe I don't just want to be safe, trapped in Taquul, dull yet protected,' she responded. 'Maybe I'd rather be at risk here with you, than anywhere else in the world.'

The words were thrown like a gauntlet. They stared at each other, the meaning behind her statement impossible to miss.

She waited, needing him to speak, but he didn't, and so she asked, quietly, her voice just a whisper, 'Do you really want me to leave, Amir?' She pressed her hand to his chest, feeling the thudding of his heart, wondering if it was beating for her.

'I *need* it.'

She shook her head, pain beginning to spread through her. Why couldn't he see what was right in front of him?

'I'm not afraid.' She tilted her chin defiantly. 'You overreacted earlier this week, when the man threw a coffee cup at me, and you're overreacting now. I'm not made of glass.'

'Overreacting? Did you not hear me, Jo? I've just had the chief of my military agency telling me to *detain you*.' A shiver ran down her spine at the ugliness of that—how quickly people could turn! 'If it turns out that this attack had *any degree* of government assistance then those calls will become louder. Here in Ishkana, to almost all of my people, you *are* the enemy.'

Stricken and pale, she trembled. His eyes swept over her, spreading nothing. No warmth. She felt cold to the core of her being.

'You will leave this morning, instead of tomorrow afternoon. Understood?'

'No!' She shook her head in a last-ditch effort to make him see things as she did—or had. She couldn't deny the kernel of fear that was spreading through her. But she had to be brave—more was at stake now. If he knew how she felt and what she wanted, would it make a difference?

'You're the one who doesn't understand. I don't want to leave now. I don't want to leave tomorrow. I want to stay here in Ishkana with you, for the rest of my life, however long that might be. Anything else is unacceptable to me.' She pressed her hands to her hips, adopting a stance that was pure courage and strength when inside she was trembling like a leaf.

His expression was impossible to interpret. Dark eyes met and held hers, and he said nothing for so long that her stance began to weaken, one hand dropping to her side, a feeling of loss spreading through her.

'It's impossible.'

'There would be difficulties,' she corrected. 'But what we have is worth fighting for.'

'If things were different,' he said quietly, his hands lifting to catch her face, cradling her cheeks as he held her so he could see everything that crossed her expression, 'I might want that too.'

It was both the bursting of light and hope within her and the breaking apart of it too. 'Things don't need to be different. I'm here with you now. Does it make any sense for me to be elsewhere?'

His eyes swept shut. 'There's no future for us, *inti qamar*. We've always known that.'

Her heart was in pain. 'Don't you see what I'm trying to tell you?'

He moved a finger to her lips. 'Don't say it.' His Adam's apple jerked as he swallowed. 'Please don't say it. I don't wish to hurt you by not answering with what you would hope to hear in return.' He padded his thumb over her lower lip.

'So then say it,' she whispered. 'I know you feel it.'

'You're wrong.' He shook his head. 'I fought this. I fought you.' He had. When she'd first come to Ishkana he'd tried so hard to stop any of this from happening. 'I should have fought harder.' He stepped back from her, and again she had the sense that he was ending the conversation, making an arbitrary decision that there was no more to say.

It violated everything she felt and wanted. She stamped her foot as he crossed to the door. He was leaving.

'I love you, Amir.' He stopped walking and stood completely still. 'I have fallen so completely in love with you, and not just you—this damned country of yours. I want to stay here with you as your wife, to live my life at your side. Whatever the risks, I want to be here with you.' His back was ramrod straight. 'I love you.'

She felt as though she were paused mid-air, waiting to have a parachute pulled or to drop like a dead weight towards earth. She didn't move. She waited, her lungs burning with the force of breathing, her arms strangely heavy.

'Loving me is—'

She held her breath.

'I don't want your love.'

She flinched.

'I will never return it.' His eyes bore into hers, the seriousness of what he was saying eclipsed by a look that showed her he meant every horrible word he said.

'Then what exactly have we been doing?'

He clamped his lips together, his jaw pressing firm. 'Not falling in love.'

She shook her head; she couldn't believe it. 'I have been.' She swallowed past a wave of bitterness. 'And nothing you say will make me change my mind on that.'

His response was to walk away from her, across the room. At the door, he turned to face her. 'Forget about me, Johara. Go home to Taquul, live your life. Be happy. Please.'

The helicopter lifted from the palace, and he watched it take off into the dawn sky. With one call he could have it summoned back to the palace. A word to a servant and the pilot would respond, bringing the helicopter—and its passenger—back to him. *I want to stay here with you as your wife.*

It was impossible.

If this morning's outbreak of violence had demonstrated anything it was that the people of Taquul and Ishkana would never tolerate anything of the sort. *Detain the Princess.*

If he weren't Sheikh? And she weren't a princess?

No. He wouldn't lose himself in hypotheticals. He was Sheikh Amir Haddad of Ishkana and his allegiance was—and always would be—to his country.

He wouldn't think of her again.

* * *

'It makes sense, Jo.'

She sat very still, listening to her brother, her eyes focussed on the spectacular view framed through the windows of this room. Desert sand, the crispest white, spread before them, meeting a sky that was a blisteringly bright blue.

It was just as it had been from the ruins.

So much of Taquul was like Ishkana.

'You must be able to see how right this is. It's what our parents wanted, it's what I want, what he wants. I think deep down it's even what you want.'

'Well,' she couldn't help drawling her response, 'I'm glad you've given what I want *some* thought, seeing as I'd be the one marrying him.'

'You used to like Paris,' Malik said with a shake of his head, coming to sit beside her. The smell of his tea reached her nostrils.

'I still like Paris,' she agreed. 'I consider him a friend. But I don't intend to marry him.'

Malik sighed. 'What's got into you?'

She turned to face him, her eyes clear. 'What do you mean?'

'You've been…different…since you got back from Ishkana.'

Got back. Returned. Came 'home'. All perfectly calm ways to describe the fact she felt as though a rocket had blasted her world into pieces.

'I felt the same way about this before I left. I have never intended to marry Paris. Not really.' She sighed. 'I can see the sense of it. I can tell it's what you want, and yes, I can see why. But I won't marry him.'

'He cares for you.'

I love you. He hadn't said anything back. Did that mean he didn't love her? Or that he *couldn't* love her?

It didn't matter. Four weeks had passed. Four weeks. With effort, work and a lot of the reason, sympathy and diplomacy Johara had advocated for, peace was being forged, and it was strengthening with every day that passed. Life was normal again. Except it wasn't. In the middle of her chest there was an enormous black hole. She went through the motions each day, imitating the woman she'd once been. But while her body had returned to Taquul, her heart and soul had remained behind in Ishkana. She doubted the two would ever reunite.

'I can't marry him,' she said, more strenuously.

'Why not?'

Why not? The truth was screaming through her. She stood uneasily, jerkily, moving to the window. The maze was around the corner. If she leaned forward, she'd be able to see just a hint of its verdant walls. She closed her eyes, nausea rising inside her.

'I *am* different.' The words were barely a whisper. She heard the rustle of clothing as her brother came to stand behind her. 'Something happened in Ishkana and it's changed me. I might have been more malleable once. I might even have agreed to this, to please you, and because yes, I can see that it makes a sort of sense. But not now. I can't. Please don't ask me again.'

'What happened, Jo?' There was urgency in his question. 'Did someone hurt you?' She heard the fear beneath the statement. Why couldn't they stop worrying about her? As though she were so fragile, and couldn't look after herself.

'I was treated as an honoured guest,' she assured him. 'No one hurt me.'

And because the words had been pressing down on her like an awful weight for a month now, she said them aloud, needing to speak them to make them real, and to understand them better. 'I fell in love.' She angled her face towards her brother's. 'I fell in love in Ishkana. The idea of marrying Paris—or anyone—makes my blood run cold. Please don't ask it of me.'

'Fell in love?' he repeated, frowning, as though this was an entirely foreign concept. 'With whom?'

Was there any sense in lying? She bit down on her lip, searching for what she should say or do.

But Malik swore, shook his head. 'No. Not him.'

'Yes.' She twisted her fingers at her side, seeing her brother's shock and wishing she hadn't been the instrument of it, and also not caring, because inside she'd grown numb and cold.

'Johara, you cannot be serious.'

She bit down on her lip. 'I love him.'

'This man is—he is—'

'What is he?' she challenged defiantly, anger coursing through her veins. 'The war is over.'

'But the sentiments are not.' He sighed angrily. 'We were at war a long time. You might be ready to forget that but our people won't. There's been too much loss. Too much hurt. It's going to take time and you, a princess of Taquul, cannot simply do as you wish.'

'Of course I can.' She held his gaze levelly, her expression firm. 'I refuse to be bound by a war that has ended, by a war that was started a century ago. I refuse to hate a man I hadn't even met until a few weeks ago. I love him—and you cannot, will not, change my mind or my heart.'

Malik glared at her with a mix of outrage and disbelief. 'I forbid it. I forbid any of this. You will marry Paris and that's the end of it.'

He stared at her for several more seconds then turned, stalking towards the door. He slammed it behind him; she didn't so much as flinch.

Amir told himself he wouldn't ask about her. This day wasn't about Johara. It wasn't about him. This was an event marking six months of hard-fought-for peace, a meeting with Malik Qadir, to show the world that the two leaders were intent on progressing matters. It hadn't been smooth sailing, but each little outbreak had been quickly quelled. All-out war had been avoided.

'Let me stand by your side. Let them see us united.'

He heard her voice often. Her promises. Her offer. Her desire.

'I love you.'

He wouldn't ask about her.

Within minutes, this would be over. A handshake in front of the media, and then they'd slip into their separate cars, go in separate directions, lead separate lives. Because they were Qadir and Haddad and that was what they did.

Malik had her eyes.

Amir felt as though he'd been punched in the gut. But hadn't it been that way since she'd left?

The documents were signed—more trade agreements, a relaxation on sanctions, the beginning of an economic alliance that would strengthen both countries. The business was concluded.

'Leave us.' Amir surveyed the room, encompassing Taquul and Ishkana aides in his directive.

Malik gave a single nod to show his agreement.

There was the scraping of chairs, the sound of feet against tiles, the noise as the door opened to the corridor beyond, and then they were alone; silence fell once more.

'The agreement is in order.' Malik's voice was firm. 'Our people will benefit from this.'

Amir nodded. He wouldn't ask about her.

'And it is timely too,' Malik said, standing, extending his hand to bring the meeting to an end.

If he was going to ask, it would need to be now. *How is she?* The words ran through his head, demanding an answer. He needed to know as he needed to breathe. Nothing more—just *how is she*? Was she happy?

So much of his own happiness depended on that.

'My attention can now be given over to the details of my sister's marriage.' Malik said the words simply, without any hint of malice. He couldn't have known that his statement was an instrument of intense pain to Amir. He kept his face neutral, but his body was tense, like a snake ready to strike.

'Marriage?'

'Yes.' Simple, with a smile. No ulterior motive. 'You met her fiancé, Paris.'

Amir nodded, standing, his chest constricting. 'Yes, of course. When is the wedding to take place?'

'Next week.' He held his hand out for Amir to shake. Amir stared at Malik's hand for several seconds, a frown on his face. He wanted to say so much! He wanted to ask questions, to know everything.

But he didn't have any right to ask.

'Wish…her well from me.'

A week came and went. Amir kept busy. He worked twenty-hour days, involving himself in every single ministerial portfolio. Very little went on that concerned his people of which he was not aware. He reviewed education initiatives, went through medical funding with a fine-tooth comb, oversaw high-level military meetings, and all the while he refused to pay attention to the days that were passing. He wouldn't think about Johara.

He didn't deserve to think of her.

She had offered herself to him—her heart,

her love, her service to his country—she had given him everything she had to give and he had told her to go. He'd told her to have a happy life. And that was what she was doing—with Paris.

He couldn't think about what she would have looked like on her wedding day; would she have smiled as she walked down the aisle? Was she nervous? Excited? Was she truly happy?

He couldn't think about what would happen after. Man and wife, the life they'd lead. He couldn't think about her being kissed by another man, touched by him. He couldn't think about any of it.

He'd made his decision, and even as he'd told her to leave he'd known he would regret it. He'd expected this. He owed it to both of them to hold the course.

This was for the best.

'Did they ever tell you how they met?'

Amir frowned, lifting his gaze from the wedding portrait of his parents, a decoration that had sat on his desk for so long he barely looked at it any more, focussing on Ahmed. The older man had been leaving, their meeting concluded. In fact, Amir had thought he had already left.

'No.' Amir shook his head. 'They didn't.'

'I'm not surprised.' Ahmed's smile showed

affection, but something else—strain. His eyes swept over Amir.

'I was only twelve when they died. It wasn't something we'd discussed.'

'It was the night your father's engagement was supposed to be announced.'

Amir frowned. 'They hadn't met before?'

'No.' Ahmed moved to the photo, picking it up off the desk and looking at it thoughtfully. 'She was a guest at the party, the cousin of a diplomat. Your father bumped into her—spilled a drink on her skirt, if I remember correctly—and the rest was history.'

'You're saying he was supposed to marry someone else until that night?'

'I'm saying within half an hour of meeting your mother he insisted the engagement agreement be set aside. They were inseparable.' Ahmed sighed.

Amir held his hand out, and Ahmed put the photo in it. The happiness in his parents' eyes was palpable. Through the veil of time he could feel the joy that had been captured in this moment.

'I know how happy they were,' Amir agreed.

'Yes. They were happy.' Ahmed frowned, sighed heavily once more, so Amir looked towards the older man with a frown, wondering what was on his mind. 'I often think about that.

Would they have changed anything if they'd known what would happen?'

Amir stiffened in his seat, replacing the photo on the edge of his desk with care. 'It's impossible to know.'

'No.' Ahmed's smile was wistful. 'It's not. I believe that even if they'd been told on their wedding day what fate awaited them, they would not have shied away from it. Not when it brought you, and the time they had together.'

Amir's chest felt tight.

'I'm sorry, Your Majesty. At my age, the brain tends to become reflective.'

Ahmed moved towards the door. Before he could open it, Amir said, 'My mother paid a high price for that happiness.'

Ahmed frowned. 'I think if she was here she'd say it was worth it.'

Amir often dreamed of his parents. That they were drowning, or on fire, or falling from a cliff, and in every dream he reached for them, his fingertips brushing the cotton of his mother's clothes, or the ends of her hair, grabbing without holding, so close but ultimately ineffectual.

He knew what was at the root of the dreams: a disbelief that he hadn't been able to save them. A desire to go back to that night and do something, anything, that would change the twist of fate that had taken them from him.

His powerlessness had sat about his shoulders for a long time, and he'd never really accepted it.

This dream was different. Johara, in a maze. Not like the maze in Taquul, this had white walls, and as she ran through it the corridors became narrower and narrower, so that he could never reach her. Whenever he got close, she'd slip away again, disappearing no matter how hard he looked.

He woke with a start, his breath rushed, his forehead covered in perspiration.

She's getting married.

'I love you.'

'I want to stay here with you.'

He swore. Anger flooded his body. He ached for her. He felt her everywhere he looked, but she was gone.

He hadn't been able to catch her; he'd failed her.

CHAPTER THIRTEEN

BEING BACK IN Manhattan was a balm. It was temporary, but it was enough. She stifled a yawn with the back of her hand, glad the evening—the launch of a new therapy space and classroom funded by her charity—had been a success. And for a brief moment, as she'd walked through the room and smiled and spoken to the assembled guests, she'd almost felt like herself again.

Almost.

It was impossible to forget. It was impossible to feel whole when so much of herself was locked away in a space she couldn't access. She'd stopped counting the days since she'd left Ishkana. When it had passed ninety, she'd known: it was too long. He wasn't going to change his mind—he was glad she'd left. He'd forgotten about her. He'd drawn boundaries for their relationship and he was sticking to them with a determination that was innate to him.

Day by day she'd concentrated on Taquul, on taking on a role there, on seeming as though she were fine and focussed on a life that no longer held any appeal for her. She didn't speak about Ishkana or Amir, not even with her brother, and Malik never asked. At least he'd dropped the matter of her marrying Paris—for now. She went through the motions, day in, day out, breathing, eating, sleeping, smiling, when inside she felt as though she were withering and dying.

She used to try not to think of Amir but that was ludicrous—like trying to stop one's heart from beating. It was something she did reflexively so now she didn't even bother to fight it. She accepted that he would always be a part of her, even when he wasn't. She accepted that she would always look for him, think of him, reach for him—and that she'd never again see him or touch him.

Pain was her constant companion, but so what? She could live with it; she would live with it, because even pain was a reminder of him. And in the meantime, she could still make something of her life. She would always know that he was missing, but she refused to be cowed by that. In time, she'd grow strong again.

Perhaps she was already strong? She'd refused Malik's attempts to organise her marriage. She'd come to New York when he'd clearly wished her to stay. She was carving out the best life she could. And one day, she'd be happy again. Never complete, but content.

She had to be. There had been too much loss, grief, sadness and death for her to waste her life. She wouldn't allow herself to indulge in misery.

Her car pulled to a stop outside the prestigious high rise she called home while in the States, her security guard coming to open her door. She ignored the overt presence of guards flanking the door—the apartment was home to many celebrities and powerful politicians; such security measures were normal. Her guards walked her through the lobby. She barely noticed them.

Almost home now, she let the mask slip for a moment, allowing herself to feel her loneliness and solitude without judgement. The elevator doors pinged open and she stepped inside. One of her guards went with her, as was protocol, but before the doors closed another man entered. Unmistakably, he was of a security detail, but not hers.

A second later, the walls seemed to be closing in on her as a second man entered the elevator. Johara couldn't breathe. Her eyes had stars in them. She pressed her back to the wall of the elevator, sure she was seeing things, or that she'd passed out and conjured Amir from the relics of her soul, because he couldn't possibly be right in front of her, inside the elevator, here in Manhattan?

His dark eyes glowed with intent, his face a forbidding mask that made her knees tremble and her stomach tighten. She opened her mouth to ask him something—to ask if it was really him—but she couldn't. No words would form.

'I'd like a meeting with Her Highness.' He addressed his comment to her guard.

Her stomach flipped.

The guard looked to her. She could see his doubts—the peace was new. He didn't want to offend this powerful sheikh, but nor could he consent to this highly improper request.

She had to say something. A thousand questions flooded her. Anger, too. What was he doing here? Why had he come? It had been too long. Too long! Didn't he see how she'd changed? Couldn't he tell that inside, behind the beautiful dress and the make-up and the hair, she was like a cut flower left in the sun too long? She angled her face away from his. In the circumstances, his handsome appearance was an insult. How dared he look so good? So virile? So strong and healthy, as though he hadn't missed a moment's sleep since she left?

'I'm tired,' she said—the words ringing with

honesty because they were accurate. She was exhausted.

'Yes.' It was quiet. Sympathetic. He *could* see what she hid from the rest of the world. He could see inside her heart and recognise its brokenness.

She swallowed, hurting so much more now that he was here. The elevator doors closed but the carriage didn't move. Not until Amir reached across and pressed a button.

'This is important.'

Resistance fired through her. What she'd said to him, the night she'd left, had been important too. He hadn't listened. He'd made up his own mind and nothing she'd said could change it. She'd told him she loved him and he'd turned his back on her as though she meant nothing.

'I'm tired,' she said again, shaking her head. Her guard moved closer, as though to protect her. Amir stiffened and waved away his own guard. Most people wouldn't have noticed, but she was attuned to every movement he made. She saw the tiny shift of his body, the strengthening of every muscle he possessed.

His gaze bore into hers; she knew he registered everything she felt, and she didn't try to hide it. She returned his stare unflinchingly, because she wanted him to feel what he'd done to her. It was petty but necessary.

A muscle jerked in his jaw and a moment later he nodded, a look of acceptance on his features. 'Tomorrow, then.'

Her stomach squeezed. Tomorrow felt like a year away. She'd never sleep if she knew he wanted to speak to her. What could he possibly have to say?

It had been too long.

She bit down on her lip and damn it! Tears filled her eyes. She blinked rapidly, clearing them as best she could.

'We don't have any business together, Your Majesty.' The words were shaky. 'If it's a state concern, there are more appropriate channels—'

'It isn't.'

She had to press her back to the wall, needing its support. The elevator stopped moving and Amir's guard stepped out, keeping one hand pressed to hold the doors open.

'This is a private matter.' His eyes didn't leave her face. 'This level is my apartment. Here is the key to my room. I'll stay until five p.m. tomorrow. If you find you would like to hear what I have to say, then come to me. Any time, Johara. I will wait.'

She stared at the key as though it were a poisonous snake, her fingertips twitching, her heart aching, her brain hurting.

'It's your decision,' he said quietly, and the

gentleness of the promise had her reaching for the key.

She didn't say anything. She didn't promise anything. She couldn't. She felt blindsided, utterly and completely.

He turned and swept out of the elevator, but he was still there, even as the doors closed and it crested one level higher. She could smell him. She could feel him. Just knowing he was in the same building was filling her body with an ancient pounding of a drum, or the rolling in of the sea, waves crashing against her, making her throb with awareness, need, hurt, pain, love, and everything in between.

At three in the morning, she gave up trying to sleep. She pushed out of bed and walked towards the window, staring out at the glistening lights of New York. Even at this hour, the city exuded a vibrancy she'd always found intoxicating. But not now.

She barely saw the lights. All she could think about was Amir. Was he staring out at the same view? Thinking about her? Why was he here?

This is a private matter.

What could that mean?

Her heart slammed into her ribs—hard—then she turned back to the bed, looking at the table beside it. His key sat there, staring right back at her.

Her heart flipped.

What was she doing?

Instead of standing here asking an empty bedroom why he was there and what he wanted, she could go down and demand he tell her. That made more sense.

Before she could second-guess herself, she grabbed her silken robe and wrapped it around herself, cinching it at the waist, then reached for the key. There was no risk of being seen by a nosy guest or paparazzi; she had the whole level of the building.

At his door, she hesitated for the briefest moment. She lifted a hand to knock, then shook her head, pressing the key to the door, pushing it inwards as she heard the buzz.

It was immediately obvious that he wasn't asleep. The lounge area was dimly lit. He sat in an armchair, elbows pressed to his knees, face looking straight ahead. The moment she entered, he stood, his body tense, his expression dark.

He wasn't surprised though. He'd been waiting for her. The realisation made her stomach clench.

'Why are you here?' It was the question she most desperately needed an answer to.

'To see you.'

It was the answer she wanted and yet it wasn't. It gave her so little.

She moved deeper into the apartment, the similarities to hers in its layout disorientating at first.

'Why?'

More was needed. More information. More everything.

'Please, sit down.'

She eyed the armchair warily, shaking her head. She felt better standing.

'Would you like a drink?'

She made a groaning noise of impatience. 'Amir, tell me…'

He nodded. He understood. He crossed to her, but didn't touch her. She could sense the care he took with that, keeping himself far enough away that there was no risk of their fingers brushing by mistake.

'I came to New York because it was the easiest way to see you.'

She frowned.

'Your brother would not send you back to Ishkana.'

She swallowed.

'You invited me?'

'No. But after he lied about your marriage

to Paris, I read between the lines. You told him about us.'

Her jaw dropped. 'He what?'

'He told me you were to be married. At first I believed it to be true.'

She shook her head. 'He was wrong to do that. I never agreed. I would never agree.'

'I know.' His tone was gentle, calming. But she didn't feel calm. Frustration slammed through her.

'You told him about us, and he doesn't approve.'

She ground her teeth together. 'Whether he does or doesn't is beside the point. Malik has nothing to do with us.'

He studied her for several long seconds.

'He's your brother,' Amir said quietly.

'Yes. But I'm a big girl and this is my life. I make my own decisions.'

'I wanted to see you,' Malik said quietly. 'But arranging a visit to Taquul and coinciding our schedules proved difficult. Particularly without alerting anyone to the purpose of my visit.'

'Yes, I understand that.' She frowned.

'When I heard you were coming to New York, I followed.'

I followed. Such sweet words; she couldn't let them go to her head.

'Why?'

His smile was a ghost on his face. His eyes traced a line from the corner of her eye to the edge of her lips and she felt almost as though he were touching her. She trembled.

'Before you left Ishkana, I should have explained everything better. Only I didn't understand myself then. I couldn't see why I acted as I did. It took losing you, missing you, hearing that you were to marry someone else and knowing myself to be at the lowest ebb of my life only to pass through sheer euphoria at the discovery that you were not married. It took all these things for me to understand myself. I couldn't explain to you that night, because I didn't know.'

She swayed a little, her knees unsteady.

'I didn't ever decide to push you away. I never consciously made that decision, but it's what I've been doing all my life, or since my parents died at least. I have many people that consider me a friend yet I do not rely on anyone. Not because I don't trust them but because I don't trust life.' His smile was hollow. 'I lost my parents and I have been permanently bracing to experience that grief all over again. Until I met you, I shielded myself the only way I knew how—I made sure I never cared about anyone enough to truly feel their absence.'

Her stomach felt as though it had dropped

right to the ground outside. Sadness welled up inside her. 'That sounds very lonely.'

'Loneliness is not the worst thing.' He brushed her sympathy aside. 'But you made it impossible to not care. I tried so hard not to love you, and yet you became a part of me.' He stopped talking abruptly, the words surprising both of them. 'Losing you would have been almost the worst thing that could happen to me—feeling that pain again would have been crippling. But so much worse if it were my fault. When you told me you wanted to stay with me, as my wife, I wanted to hold you so close and never let you go—but what if? What if something happened to you, and all because of my selfishness?'

Her heart was splintering apart for him. His fears were so understandable, but all this heartbreak…

'And I'm a Qadir,' she said quietly, trying to hold onto a hint of the bitterness that had been their stock in trade for generations.

He returned her stare unflinchingly. 'You're the woman I love.'

Her breath caught.

'And I am still half terrified that my love will ruin you, but I have realised something very important in the long months since you left the palace.'

She waited, impatient, desperate.

'You were right that night. This should have been your decision. You know what the risks are to our marriage, and you know that it will change many things for you, including, perhaps, your relationship with your brother. But these are your choices to make, not mine. I pushed you away, as I push everyone away, because that seemed better than taking this gamble. Yet it isn't mine to take.'

His voice was deep, gravelled.

'Only let me assure you that if you wish to make your life with me, I will do everything within my power to keep you safe and make you happy.'

She was silent. Dumbfounded.

'I know I hurt you.' Now, finally, he touched her. The lightest brush of his fingertips to hers. 'It was something I swore I wouldn't do yet in trying to protect you that's exactly what happened.'

She tilted her face away, tears stinging her eyes. 'You did hurt me,' she agreed softly. 'You pushed me away at a time when you could have used my support. You made me irrelevant. You're not the first person to do that, but it hurt the worst with you because I expected so much more.'

He groaned. 'I acted on instinct.'

She bit down on her lip, nodding. 'And I went

home, and I waited, and I thought of you, and I have missed you every single day and you've been nowhere. It was as though it never happened. And now you're asking me to forget, and feel as I did then?' Her heart was battered and mangled and yet it was also bursting. Her defiant speech felt good to throw at him, but it wasn't really how she felt. She watched her words hit their mark, the pain in his face, the apology she felt in his eyes.

'I came here knowing you might not want what you did then. But still I had to explain. I didn't ask you to leave because I didn't love you. I loved you too much to have you stay. And I love you now, too much to fight you. Just know that you will always be my reason for being, Johara. Whether you're with me or not, everything I do will be for you.'

He lifted her hand to his lips and kissed it lightly, and she tilted her head back to his, facing him. 'I love you.'

He offered the words so simply, and they pushed inside her, shaking her out of the state she was in. This was really happening. He was standing in front of her pouring his heart out and she was holding onto the anger she'd felt. Was she doing exactly the same thing he had? Pushing him away because she was scared of being hurt again?

Maybe love always brought with it a sense of danger—and the gamble made the pay-off so much sweeter.

'So what are you saying?' she asked quietly, surprised her voice sounded so level when her insides were going haywire.

'Is that not obvious?'

She shook her head. 'I think I need you to say it.'

He nodded, his Adam's apple shifting as he swallowed. 'I wish I could go back to that night and change everything I said and did. I wish I had pulled you into my arms, thanked you for what you were offering and walked hand in hand with you to deal with the problems that faced *us*. Not me. *Us*. About *our* countries.' Her lips parted as she drew in a shaky breath.

'But I cannot go back in time, and I cannot change what I did then. So I am promising you my heart, and my future, and everything I can share with you. I am asking you to marry me, if you can find it in your heart to forgive me. I am asking you to be not just my wife, and the mother of my children, but a ruler at my side. You are brilliant and brave and your instincts are incredible. I would be lucky to have you as my wife, and Ishkana would be blessed to have you as its Queen. I'm asking you to look beyond the past to the future that we could have. And in exchange I promise that I will never again fail you. I will never again fail to see your strength and courage, to understand what you are capable of.'

Tears fell unchecked down her cheeks now. He caught one with the pad of his thumb, then another, wiping her face clean.

'Don't cry.' The words were gruff. 'Please.'

She laughed, though, a half-sob, a sign of how broken and fixed she felt all at once.

'Damn it, Amir, I wanted to hate you,' she said, stamping her foot. 'I have missed you so much.'

'I know.' He groaned, pulling her towards him, holding her close to his body. 'That is mutual.'

She listened to his heart and knew that it was beating for her, just as it always had. She stayed there with her head pressed to his chest, listening, believing, adjusting to the reality she was living, to the happiness that was within reach. They both had to be brave, but the alternative was too miserable to contemplate.

She blinked up at him, smiling. 'Let's go home, Amir.'

He made a growling sound of relief, pleasure, delight, and then he swooped his lips down to kiss her. 'Yes, *inti qamar*. Let us go home.'

* * *

'You can't be serious.'

Amir couldn't take his eyes off Johara. Through the glass of his bedroom, he watched her sleeping and felt as though nothing and no one could ever hurt him. She was here, in Ishkana, where she belonged. Seven months ago he'd pushed her away, believing the best thing he could do for her was arrange safe passage to Taquul. How wrong he'd been. And how fortunate he was that her heart was so forgiving...

'We flew back a few hours ago.' Behind him, the sun was beginning to break into the sky. 'It's all agreed.'

'You cannot marry her. I forbid it.'

'Your lack of consent will hurt Jo, Malik, but it will do nothing to change our plans.'

Silence met his pronouncement. If the past had taught them anything it was that neither wanted to risk another outbreak of violence. They both knew the cost too well. Malik might be furious, but he would not threaten military action.

'You must have kidnapped her. Taken her against her will.'

Amir straightened at the very suggestion. 'I will never, in my life, do *anything* against your sister's will. She came here because we are in love, Malik, as you are well aware.' The gentle rebuke sat between them. It was the reason, after all, that Malik had lied about an impending marriage to Paris.

'Love,' Malik spat with disbelief. 'She is a princess of Taquul. Her place is here.'

'Her place,' Amir corrected with a smile that came from deep within his heart, 'is wherever she wants it to be.'

Inside, Johara caught the statement through the open door, her eyes blinking open. She listened, her breath in a state of suspension as the man she intended to spend the rest of her life with spoke to—she could only presume—her brother.

'I insist on speaking to her.'

'Yes, of course,' Amir agreed. 'She is still asleep, but I have no doubt she will wish to speak to you about this. The purpose for my call is simple—I wanted to alert you to the state of affairs and to caution you against saying or doing anything to upset her.'

'Is that a threat?'

'A threat? No. It's a promise. If you push her away, you will lose her completely, Malik. She has chosen where she wants to be, and with whom.' He sighed. 'I love your sister. I plan to make her very happy by giving her everything she could ever want—and we both know that is for us to be, if not exactly friends, capable of existing harmoniously.'

Silence met this statement.

'She and I are to marry. She will carry my children, the heirs to Ishkana. They will be your nieces and nephews. Can you think of anyone who will benefit from continued estrangement?'

Inside the bedroom, Johara smiled, her eyes fluttering closed. She was exactly where she wanted to be and, with all her heart, she knew that the decision she'd made had been the right one. The only one she could ever make. Her heart, the skies, fate and future had guided her here—it was where she was meant to be.

EPILOGUE

AMIR HAD BEEN WRONG. He had believed his people, and the people of Taquul, would revolt at the very idea of a union between himself and Johara. He had braced for that, and prepared Johara for the inevitable splashback.

There had been none.

Nothing but euphoric delight and anticipation. Every detail of their union was discussed at length. He could not turn on the television without catching some talk-show host speculating about which tiara she would wear down the aisle, and whether the jewel for her ring would be of Taquul or Ishkana.

Billboards were pasted across the city with a smiling photo of Johara, welcoming her to Ishkana. Despite the pain his people had felt—or perhaps because of it—they welcomed her, knowing that lasting peace was truly at hand. With this marriage, the war became impossible. Their union bonded the countries in a way no peace treaty alone ever could. They were family now. His children would be a mix of them, and of their countries, and he had every intention of their being raised in the light of both countries and cultures.

Separation was not the way forward. Unity was. Just as Johara had said.

In the end, she wore a tiara that had belonged to her mother, and a wedding ring that had been his mother's. Her dress was made of spider's silk, lace and beads, and when she walked towards him, he felt as though it were just him and her, and no one else in the world. When she walked towards him, he felt as though he might be about to soar into the heavens.

She smiled at him and he felt a thousand and one things—gladness, love, pleasure, relief, and a small part of him felt sorrow that his parents would never know her. But in a way, their happiness would be a part of this, because through their example he'd finally understood that being fearless was a necessity to love.

A year after their wedding, to the day, they were blessed with the birth of a son. Two years later, twin daughters followed. And for all the years into the future they'd hoped for, peace, happiness and prosperity favoured not only

Amir and Johara, but the people of their kingdoms as well.

There was, as it turned out, never a story with less woe than that of Amir and his Jo.

* * * * *

Captivated by
Their Impossible Desert Match?
*You won't be able to resist these
other stories
by Clare Connelly!*

Bride Behind the Billion-Dollar Veil
Redemption of the Untamed Italian
The Secret Kept from the King
Hired by the Impossible Greek

Available now!